CHRONICLES OF V

Bright Stars

TASCHE LAINE

SKYE BLUE PRESS

Cover Design by 100 Covers, 100covers.com

ISBN-13: 978-1-955674-13-3 (ebook)

ISBN-13: 978-1-955674-14-0 (paperback)

ISBN-13: 978-1-955674-15-7 (hardcover)

Library of Congress Control Number: 2021915782

Printed in the United States of America

First Edition 2023

Skye Blue Press

Vancouver, WA

https://skyebluepress.com

CONTENTS

For Peter

"There is no footprint too small to leave an imprint on this world."

— UNKNOWN

PART ONE

I

PEANUT BUTTER

I love peanut butter; it's my comfort food. Peanut butter brought me my best friend, Emma Moreno, in first grade. Peanut butter got me through her kidnapping eight years later, in ninth grade. And peanut butter would get me through this day, too. I feel for people with peanut allergies . . . I'm not sure I could live without it.

I patted my peanut butter and banana sandwich, tucked in the depths of my backpack, and swung the pack over my left shoulder. Then I squared my shoulders and sighed, looking up at Sierra High School.

I've dreaded this day all summer. It's the first day of sophomore year. The worst day of my life had been the first day of freshman year—just one year ago.

I didn't have high hopes for this first day, either. *Here we go.*

I trudged toward the main building from the staff parking lot. Since my parents were both teachers at my school, I had to go to school early every day—*yay me.* I slowed my steps even more (a snail would be proud) to distance myself from my parents, wishing I could drive myself to school. I'd been wanting to get my learner's permit since I'd turned fifteen in June, but my mom refused to teach me how to drive. She said she's not ready for me to drive yet—or grow up. *Whatever.*

"Good morning, Violet—em, uh, I mean, V. Did you have a pleasant summer?" asked an all-too-familiar voice ahead of me. The principal, Dr. Michael Fitzgibbon, extended his hand to greet me as I plodded up the steps. He stood at the school's entrance with a dopey smile plastered to his face.

"Hi, Dr. Fitz," I said. "Yeah, sure. You?" Charm was not my forte.

"You know, V, we've got to stop meeting like this," Dr. Fitz said, chuckling after his comment like he just told the punchline to the world's funniest joke.

"Huh?"

"Oh, you remember. Come on, don't you remember?"

I shook my head.

"I caught you running in the hallway last year. You were so nervous for your first day of high school." He paused and gazed past me, then continued in a softer voice, "You certainly have changed this past year. I bet you're looking forward to starting your sophomore year off on the right foot now. I mean, after everything you girls went through and—"

"Seriously? That's what you think? You think I gave a crap about high school when my best friend was missing? Are you kidding me right now?" *Ugh. Hold on, everybody. We're in for a wild ride.* "Look, Fitz, if you don't mind, I'd appreciate it if you'd just stop coddling me and treat me like everyone else. If one more person tells me what I 'went through' again, I'm gonna—"

"There you are, V!" Emma ran up to us, panting. "I've been looking for you everywhere. I'm sorry, Dr. Fitzgibbon. She forgot to take her meds today." Emma put her arm around me and patted me on the shoulder.

"Ha ha, very funny," I said, crossing my arms and pretending to be annoyed. But it actually surprised me to see Emma in such a good mood; I wanted to savor the moment.

"I know you're doing the best you can, V," Dr. Fitz said. "Really, I do. Just work on that short fuse a bit more, okay? Honestly, your teachers last year went easy on you. But this year, I expect you to behave. And I'm hoping you stay out of my office. Well, at least stop getting sent there for disciplinary purposes. Is that clear?"

"Yes, sir."

"Good. You ladies have a great day, okay?"

"Thank you, Dr. Fitzgibbon. We will," Emma said. She smiled sweetly and nudged me into the building, down the hall, and around the corner. She waited until we were far enough away that Dr. Fitz wouldn't hear us. Then she turned on me, emphatic. "It's the first day of school and you're already talking to him like that? Would it kill you to be a little nicer to authority figures? Geez, V, I'm tired of bailing you out."

"Then don't. Since when did I ask for your help?"

"Knock it off. That tough act doesn't work on me, and you know it. Do you think I don't know what today is? How could I not know? V, it's *me.*"

Today. The day I've been dreading. The day it all started—a year ago.

Emma had been kidnapped on her way to school at 7:07 a.m. It was a case of mistaken identity. The kidnappers meant to take another brown-eyed, raven-haired beauty, Brylee Rossi, who was two years older than us. Eventually, the kidnappers realized their mistake and abducted Brylee two weeks later.

But Emma? *My* Emma? She didn't even make it to our first

day of freshman year. She didn't even make it to our first *month* of freshman year. All our plans changed in the time it took some creep to grab her and shove her in a minivan. Our lives had irrevocably changed—forever.

I'd made it my mission to find her and get her back. And I did! I found her. I saved Brylee Rossi, too. Then I gave the police directions to find the others, so I guess I also saved them —thirty-four girls and women *I* rescued. I was a hero.

But today? I didn't feel like a hero. Since the rescue, I'd longed for things to go back to normal, to the way they were *before*. We were happy then. But our lives will never be normal. The piece of our childhood they ripped away from us attests to that.

"I'm sorry, Emma," I whispered, then let out a long sigh. "As usual, I'm being selfish and self-centered."

"No, you're not. I get it. It's okay—"

"I'm not finished," I interrupted. "Of course you know what today is. How could you not? It's gotta be tons harder on you than it is on me. I mean, I wasn't the one who got kidnapped, locked up for a month, and forced to . . ." I trailed off. I couldn't say what I thought had happened to her. She'd never talked to me about it. The fact was Emma didn't talk to me about much at all anymore.

"Forced to what, V? I told you I don't talk about it because there's nothing to talk about. Now drop it. Let's just go to class, okay? What do you have first period?"

"I told you yesterday when we picked up our schedules."

"Really? Hmm, I forgot. So are you going to tell me again or not?"

"Why are you mad at *me*? What did I do?" I crossed my arms, preparing for another argument.

"I'm not mad at you. Forget it. Just go to class. I'll see you later." Emma slung her backpack over her shoulder and turned to walk away.

"Applebottom," I said. I wanted a few more minutes with my best friend, who barely talked to me these days.

"What?"

"I have Computer Science with Mr. Applebottom."

"Whoa, what a funny name." She scrunched up her nose the way she used to when she was happy.

I miss that face. I miss those times.

"Right? I wonder if he's as funny as his name. What do you think?" I tried to keep it going, keep her talking.

"Don't know, but I'm sure you'll find out soon enough. I want to get to my AP Euro class a little early. I hear Mr. Feta is super strict and starts lecturing the moment the tardy bell rings. I want to make sure I sit in the front row, so I can concentrate on his lectures. I heard he takes 90 percent of his tests straight from his lectures. So I have to take good notes. Well, I better get going. I'll see ya later, V. Have a good first day, 'kay?"

And she was gone.

✦ ✦ ✦ ✦ ✦

"Miss Jiménez? Violet Jiménez?"

"Hmm? What?"

The class laughed.

"Miss Jiménez, I asked you about your mother. Her cancer is in remission, is it not?"

Seriously? He's asking me this in front of the entire class? Some people are totally clueless. "Yes, she's fine. She works here, you know. You could just ask her yourself," I shot back.

"Well, she's in the English building, and our paths don't

really cross," Mr. Applebottom said. "I merely wanted to convey my good wishes."

Great. Here I go again, overreacting and making a terrible impression in my first class of the day. What's next, getting all my teachers to hate me like they did last year? Dr. Fitz was right. This is a fresh start. I need to get a grip!

"Ahem. Well, good morning, ladies and gentlemen, my name is Mr. Applebottom, and this is Computer Science Principles. You may wonder why an old codger like me is teaching Computers. Easy enough. I drew the short straw."

Laughter.

"You don't believe me? Well, let's just say that back in my day we had stone tablets and chisels. You know, before the invention of typewriters."

"Wow! You were born before typewriters? Whoa! How old are you?" a wide-eyed freshman asked. Actually, most of the class was composed of freshmen because it was a required freshman class. I hadn't taken Computers last year because I couldn't fit it in my schedule and still take French.

Mr. Applebottom shook his head and chuckled. Then he nodded slightly and said, "Sarcasm, my dear boy. Sarcasm. The first typewriter dates all the way back to July 23, 1829. I, however, am a mere sixty-four years young." Mr. Applebottom had white hair, pale skin, and age spots. He wore a tan cardigan sweater over a plaid button-up shirt, khaki pants, and white sneakers. He wasn't wearing glasses. "I've been teaching at this school for forty years, and this is my last year. I reckon I've taught just about every subject there is, but I taught Industrial Arts most of my career."

"What's Industrial Arts?" the same kid asked.

"Well, aren't you full of questions, young fellow. Industrial Arts got changed to wood shop during the budget cut days, then it got axed from the budget altogether. Disgrace, if you ask me." He stopped and shook his head, as if to clear a bad memory. "I'd say that's enough nonsense about me. You don't want to hear a bunch of gibberish from an old fuddy-duddy like me. Now, let's talk about the history of computers. Who can tell me who invented the personal computer?"

Several hands shot up, but then they blurted out their answers without waiting to be called on. The class came alive with chatter as they agreed or disagreed with each other. The shout-outs continued.

"Steve Jobs."

"Bill Gates."

"IBM."

"All right, all right, settle down." Mr. Applebottom raised his hands, trying to get everyone's attention. "Class, settle down, please."

A few minutes passed, but everyone soon quieted.

"My, my, I'm glad to see you're all excited and ready to learn! Those are all brilliant answers, but the true credit goes to an American named Henry Edward Roberts. He designed the Altair 8800 computer in 1974, introducing the first commercially successful personal computer."

"But that's not the first computer! My dad said the British invented the first computers. My dad works for . . ." It was that same annoying kid. *Ugh, who cares? When will this class be over already?* I stifled a yawn.

"What's your name, son?"

"Arnold White."

"Well, Mr. White, your father is correct. The English inventor Charles Babbage conceived of the first digital computer and developed plans for the Analytical Engine in the mid-1830s. But sadly, it was never completed. So there's a little controversy around the origins, but supercomputers didn't come on the scene until . . ."

I tuned out again. Can you blame me? Applebottom was funny, but I had too much on my mind to care about the history of computers.

2

STILL THE FIRST DAY

The rest of the day dragged on in an endless sea of monologues as each teacher rambled on and on about the same things. You know, things like attendance, homework, classroom rules, emergency procedures, what to do in the event of a lockdown, school shooting, earthquake, fire, or other act of violence, death, and destruction. *Good times.*

Computer class morphed into English Honors, which transformed into Algebra 2, which mutated into Chemistry Honors. After fourth period, it was time for lunch. *Finally, something I can sink my teeth into! Ha.*

I spent my entire lunch break taking small bites of my sandwich while walking all over the school, looking for Emma. I hoped to run into her 'spontaneously.' For one, the peanut butter and banana sandwich was all I had with me because I'd been in a hurry this morning and hadn't had time to grab anything else, so I tried to make it last. And the searching? Emma and I didn't have any classes together this year, so I hoped we could at least hang out during lunchtime. As I mentioned, she didn't hang out with me much anymore, and I was afraid to text her because I didn't want to seem needy.

She only "bailed me out," as she called it, because of some debt she thought she owed me. She hung out with Brylee most of last year, and I barely saw her all summer. I went to Europe with my family and missed out on whatever fun Brylee and Emma were having without me. I just wanted my best friend back.

Emma and I had been best friends since forever. Well, since the first day of first grade, anyway. We'd been inseparable all these years, and our birthdays are even on the same day, June 24th. This was the first year we'd spent our birthday apart from each other. I was in Spain this year, a bazillion miles away from Emma, who was still in Orange, California.

My family loved to travel, and every summer we always went somewhere. Emma almost always came with us. But this year was different. Since the kidnapping, everything was different. Rosa, Emma's mom, had wanted her to stay home this summer. I guess I couldn't blame her for not wanting to let Emma out of her sight again.

Also, my mom got diagnosed with breast cancer last year and had to have an emergency double mastectomy. They got all the cancer out, and my mom said she felt like she had dodged a bullet. She said she wanted to celebrate . . . so Europe it was. *Bon voyage!*

Of course, I'm thrilled my mom's cancer is gone. That was the worst. I hated seeing her so sick from all the chemo they pumped into her. Plus, all her hair had fallen out, and she looked awful. I felt powerless; there was nothing I could do to help her. . . . So, that's when I had decided to put all my energy into searching for Emma.

I had avoided my mom so much that I was in Portland

when she had to get her emergency surgery. I felt guilty that I hadn't been there for her. But I was super relieved the surgery had been a massive success. Mom had made a full recovery, her red hair had eventually grown back in, although a bit curlier than before, and now she's cancer-free! Well, the doctors say to call it "in remission." It's the same thing, if you ask me.

Yet, I still can't help but feel jealous that Emma seems to be a better friend to Brylee than she is to me, and that I missed out on hanging out with them all summer. The counselors said to give Emma time, and that she'd come around when she was ready. They said to be patient and understanding, that she had gone through a terrible ordeal, and that since Brylee had gone through it with her, they now have some kind of special bond. *Great.*

I hate myself for being jealous, but screw their *special bond.* Brylee never even freaking talks to me. She's an ice queen, practically mute. I fail to see what Emma thinks is so cool about her.

Brylee had been in my Geometry class last year. The class had consisted mostly of freshmen and a few sophomores, but Brylee was the only junior. I think she flunked it her freshman year and retook it two years later. I know I sound like an awful, judgmental, selfish human being. I'm judging Brylee for being bad at math when I have no right to judge anybody. The truth is, I hate math. It's my worst subject. I actually got a C in that class. I just really miss Emma, and I know nothing will ever be the same again.

After the kidnapping, Brylee wasn't in class much because she had so many counseling appointments. I wonder if she's taking Geometry again as a senior! Ha! Truthfully, I don't even know Brylee at all, and I can only imagine what horrific things she must have had to suffer through at the hands of those monsters. Emma had said they (the kidnappers) had treated

Brylee way worse than they'd treated her. That's the most Emma's ever told me. I feel sorry for both of them. I just wish they'd never been kidnapped at all. Then Emma and I would still be best friends, and Brylee wouldn't even know we existed.

"Heads up!" a voice called out as a drone whirred past me, blowing my hair with a rush of wind.

"What the—?" I was walking past the soccer field after school, hoping to see Emma during her soccer practice. I got lost in thought, reflecting on my awful first day and how I was alone, again. Startled out of my reverie, I clenched my fists and searched for the drone's owner. A guy loped up to me with a crooked grin on his perfect face. His dark-brown spiral curls bounced as he walked, and his blue-green eyes probed straight into my soul. Goosebumps popped up all over my skin, and I realized I recognized him.

"Hey, man, I'm so sorry about that," he said. "I just got this DJI Phantom 4 Quadcopter with a 4K video camera and haven't worked out all the maneuvers yet. Are you okay?"

"What are you doing? Why would you fly that stupid thing around people if you don't know how to use it? And why on Earth would you bring it to school, you idiot? You could have hurt someone with that thing! Of all the brain-dead, incompetent—"

"V, knock it off," Brylee said, jogging over to us.

Great. What's she doing here? I suppose she's Emma's number-one fan now. I risked a quick glance at the soccer field. Emma charged down the field toward the goalie, soccer ball firmly under her control. She gave it her all, even during practices.

Soccer was her life, and I sucked at every single sport. She used to say it was our differences that made us such great friends.

"V? Did you hear me?" Brylee stood there with her hands on her hips, looking like smoke was about to come out her ears.

I glared at her. *I can stare you down any day. Bring it.*

She ignored my menacing stare and started over, saying, "I said, that drone was at least a foot away from you. Crash doesn't deserve for you to unload all your anger issues out on him."

I unclenched and clenched my fists again, deciding whether to be offended about the "anger issues" comment or let it go. I deflected back onto the guy instead and said, "Crash? What kind of stupid name is Crash? I mean, it totally suits you, but still—"

"Shut up, V. I'm warning you. Just leave him alone and walk away," Brylee said, her icy stare searing into me. With her flowing black tresses, obsidian-like eyes, black clothing, and utter lack of warmth, she reminded me of a raven. She unnerved me. Meanwhile, Crash just stood there, eyes darting back and forth between Brylee and me like he was watching a tennis match.

"Me leave *him* alone? I'm the one just trying to walk home, minding my own business. Why are you defending him, anyway? Don't you remember this is 'skateboarder guy' who plowed into my mom last year? You know, after the Halloween rally in the parking lot. Remember?"

"Yes, V. I remember," Brylee said, enunciating each syllable. "But as you just pointed out, that happened *last year*. Let it go."

"Why should I?" I asked. "Do you like him? You do, don't you? Gross. Isn't he two years younger than you? That's like, child endangerment or something."

Brylee rolled her eyes and sighed. "Again, shut up. You don't know what you're talking about, so just do us a solid and go away."

"Fine by me." I spun around to walk off and watched Brylee run back to the bleachers. She was on the track team, and, from what I could tell, she preferred to run instead of walk just about everywhere she went.

Emma was oblivious to our little scene, scoring another goal. In a way, I envied her. I sighed and turned my head back to face the direction I was walking, but not before I crashed into, well, Crash.

My body seemed to go one way while my feet went another. I landed with a hard thud straight on my butt, knocking the wind out of me. I was embarrassed, humiliated, mortified—no words could accurately describe how I felt in that moment, my cheeks turning a bright crimson.

"I'd say this makes us even," Crash said with a smile, also splayed on the ground, with his arms and legs askew. "I ran into your mom. Now you ran into me. Truce?" He hopped up, dusted himself off, and extended his hand out to help me up.

I didn't take it. I got to my feet and brushed the dirt off my rear the best I could.

"Look, V. I know we got off on the wrong foot—uh, I guess pun intended? But allow me to introduce myself. I'm Zack Collins, and I moved here last year. The day I accidentally bumped into your mom with my skateboard was October 30th. It was my first day here. So no, I had no idea who your mom was at the time. I'm sorry about her cancer, and running into her, and, well, I'd like to make it up to you if you'll let me."

"Why do they call you Crash?"

"I'll tell you about it when I pick you up. How's Friday night?"

"Nice try, but I'm busy."

"Saturday?"

"Nope. Not interested. You should've taken the hint at 'I'm busy.' So, nice to meet you, Crash, or Zack, or whatever your name is, but I've gotta go. Let's try not to run into each other— or our family members—anymore. Okay?" I didn't wait for an answer. This time, I watched where I was going and walked away at a brisk pace, trying to get this day behind me before anything else could go wrong.

3
PUPPY OR DRIVER'S ED

At dinner, Mom and Dad swapped first-day-of-school stories about their 'amazing' students and their wonderful place of employment—my high school. My mom taught English Lit and my dad taught AP History. They've been teaching there for seventeen years, and the way they were talking, you'd think today was their first day. I picked at my food while they babbled on.

"How was your day, V?" Mom asked, after she and Dad had caught up. "Michael says he ran into you this morning."

"Michael? Who?" I said with my mouth full of spinach salad.

"You know, the school principal. Duh."

"Oh! Mom! Don't call our principal by his first name. It's weird."

"Why? He's my colleague. He calls me Hannah. What do you want me to call him? Fitz, like all the kids do?"

"No, of course not. But isn't he your boss? Oh, whatever. Call him anything you want."

"So?"

"What?"

"You didn't answer my question. How was your first day as a sophomore? Do you like your teachers?"

"Only a teacher would ask that."

"That's not true. Any concerned parent would. Well, do you?"

"You're hilarious."

"Can we get a puppy?" Scotty asked.

We all stopped and stared at Scotty, my seven-year-old brother.

"Why do you ask, sweetheart?" Mom asked in return.

"Because Alex got a puppy. He told me all about her at school today. Her name is Lucy, and they adopted her from an animal shelter. She's really soft and cuddly, and it tickles when she licks his face and—"

"Okay, okay, slow down, li'l man," Dad said. "Alex's mom is home during the day. Who would take care of the puppy when we're all at school and work?"

"Carlos, don't encourage him," Mom said.

"I'm not. I'm reasoning with him," Dad replied.

"He doesn't need to be reasoned with," Mom said. "We're not getting a puppy, Scotty."

"Aw, Mom, pleeease?" Scotty pleaded.

"Sorry, sweetie, but no. I'm afraid that's my final answer. We just don't have the time to take care of a puppy."

"I'll take care of it! I have lots of time!"

Dad stifled a chuckle.

Mom glared, and everyone looked down at their plates.

"Thanks for getting the heat off me," I whispered in Scotty's ear, messing up his hair as I got up to refill my water.

"V, stop it," Scotty said. "You know I don't like it when you mess up my hair. Now it's sticking up."

"Sorry, I like playing with your hair," I said. "It's so blond, like straw. I think it's the coolest hair ever. Way better than my stringy auburn hair."

Scotty squirmed, then tried to put his hands over my mouth. "Don't say it!"

"Say what?" I mumbled through his fingers. "That you're a mini troll?"

"Stop it!" he shouted.

"That's enough, V," Mom said. "Stop antagonizing your brother."

"What does antagonizing mean?" Scotty asked.

"She's upsetting you, making you mad. But she's only teasing, sweetie. She's your sister, and she loves you. She didn't mean to upset you." Mom gave me a look. Even though I was across the room filling my glass, I felt it. "Isn't that right, V?"

"Yeah, of course. I didn't mean anything by it, squirt."

"That's better," Scotty said. "I'd much rather you called me squirt than mini troll!"

We all laughed.

I sat back down at the table and asked, "So, who wants to teach me how to drive? I'm free now if you want to get a quick lesson in."

"Haven't we been through this?" Mom asked, rolling her eyes.

"Wow, did you just roll your eyes at me?" I paused, then tried a different tactic. "Yes, I know I've asked you to take me driving a few times. But you've always said no; both of you. I've never once been allowed behind the wheel. How am I ever going to be a productive citizen if you won't let me drive? Think of how much help I could be around here. I could pick up groceries, take Scotty to and from school, run errands, even get your dry cleaning."

"Oh, I like the sound of that," Dad said. "Remind me, why aren't we letting her drive?"

"She's not old enough," Mom answered.

"What? I'm fifteen!"

"Yes, but in this state, you have to wait until you're fifteen-and-a-half before you can get a driver's permit."

"But I can start learning before then, can't I?"

"There's no rush, sweetie. You can start driving in a few months, at your half birthday."

"But that's not until December 24th! I can't get my permit on Christmas Eve; the DMV will be closed. It's not fair."

"So you wait a couple days. You can get it during Christmas break."

"But I want to get it on the exact date of my half birthday."

"Do you realize that you just started your last three sentences in a row with 'but'? Stop arguing. We're not taking you driving until you're the legal age, less than four months away. End of discussion."

"Seriously? My 'buts' are what you're focusing on?" I rolled my eyes. "English teachers are so lame," I added under my breath.

"What did you just say to me?"

"Nothing. May I be excused now?"

"Certainly. Right after you clear the table and do the dishes."

I stood up and began stacking the plates as Mom, Dad, and Scotty filed out of the dining room. Scotty shrugged as he walked past me and said, "Maybe I'll get a puppy when you get to drive."

I smiled and said, "Yeah, maybe. Mini troll."

"I heard that!" he called out from the living room. For a little kid, he was okay. Mostly.

I COULDN'T LET it go. In Computer class the next morning, I was still bothered that Mom wouldn't let me drive. By the time she finally let me, I'd still have to wait to get my permit because of having to pass a written knowledge test first. *There must be another way.*

Our school had old, clunky desktop computers in a computer lab, instead of individual laptops like my friends in private schools had. While Mr. Applebottom explained our assignment, something about writing a program and learning HTML code, I took advantage of the blinking cursor in front of me and did a quick Internet search on "driving schools."

Since Mom and Dad refused to teach me, I decided I'd pay for someone else to do it. Surprisingly, there were quite a lot to choose from. *Who knew driver training schools were such big business? Hmm, these are expensive. Where am I going to get the money for this?*

"Whatcha doin'?" Crash asked, appearing behind me.

I minimized my screen and turned around to glare at him before whispering, "What are you doing here?"

"Same as you. Duh. I'm in this class, too," he said.

"I don't remember seeing you yesterday."

"That's because I don't sit up front with the overachievers."

"I'm not an overachiever."

"Sure, V. Whatever. Hey, you're—"

"Why didn't you say we had this class together yesterday?"

"Actually, I tried to tell you, but you blew me off."

"That's not true. You asked me out, and then I blew you off." I felt my face reddening and hoped he didn't notice. *Why am I blushing?*

I faced the computer monitor again.

"Would it have made a difference if I'd tried to talk to you first?"

"Nope."

"Exactly. So I was right. You were going to blow me off no matter what I said."

I glanced down at my keyboard. After a pause I asked, "What do you want?"

"You're looking for a cheap Driver's Ed school, right?"

"Maybe. What's it to you?"

"I know a great one! Want me to tell you about it?"

"I, um . . ."

"Miss Jiménez, Mr. Collins, perhaps you could wait until I dismiss class to carry on your conversation, hmm?" Mr. Applebottom said.

I sunk into my chair, face reddening once again, while clicking the "log off" on the web browser. All I could manage was a slight nod.

"Yes, sir," Crash said. "Sorry, I was just asking V for help with our assignment. I think I missed something in my notes. Thanks, V. That was very helpful. Here are your notes back." He handed me a folded piece of paper and went back to his seat.

After Mr. Applebottom went back to his desk, I unfolded the piece of paper and read the note.

Zack (Crash) Collins (714) 555-5620.
Text me and I'll send you the info.

I stared at it, wondering if I could trust this Crash person. *Or should I call him Zack? Nah.*

4
KIND ACTS

I raced out of class as soon as the bell rang, putting distance between Crash and me before texting him. I didn't know if I wanted him to have my number, but I wanted to learn to drive, so I took the risk. My trust and faith in people these days was shady, at best. I pulled out my phone and sent him a quick text before heading into English. Miss Torres had a strict 'no cell phones allowed' policy.

> Hi, it's V. Now you have my number. Don't abuse it or I'll block you. So tell me about this great, cheap driving school.

I slipped my phone into a side pocket of my backpack and entered the classroom. Before I even made it to my seat, I felt the familiar vibration. I sat down and eased the phone out, keeping it under the desk. I clicked it on and read the new text.

> Trust issues much? What's the magic word?

Ugh. What is it with this guy? I texted my reply.

P-L-E-A-S-E

The tardy bell rang. I glanced down at my phone again as it vibrated in my hand.

As you wish! Haha. It's called Dan's Driving Instruction. I think it's www.ddi.com. If that doesn't work, it'll come up in the name search.

I'll check it out. Thanks.

"Violet?" Miss Torres said. She walked down the aisle and stood in front of me, inches away from my desk. "Put your phone away. Since it's only the second day of school, that's your one warning. The next time, I'll take it and you can have it back at the end of the day."

"The end of the day? That's not fair!" I protested.

"Would you like to forgo the warning and hand it over now, then?"

"No, I'll take the warning. I'm putting it away." I bent over and put my phone in my backpack's side pocket before she changed her mind.

"Good. Then you won't have to worry about having it taken, will you?"

"I guess."

"You guess? I see. Violet, I'd like to have a word with you after class. Please remain seated when the bell rings."

Great. Here we go again.

WHEN THE BELL RANG, Miss Torres stared at me while she dismissed the class. Her eyes bore into me as if daring me to get out of my seat. I remained seated and waited, dreading whatever was about to spew out of her mouth.

"So, I bet you think this is about the phone thing," Miss Torres said, sitting down in the desk across from mine.

"Isn't it?" I asked, meeting her gaze.

"No, V, it isn't." She tucked her sable brown hair behind her ears and cleared her throat, as if collecting her thoughts.

What is going on? Is she nervous? This is so weird.

She looked at me with a slight, closed-mouth smile. I studied her face. She had kind eyes, the same dark shade that matched her hair. Her features softened as she spoke in a hushed tone. "When I was your age, my dad died of lung cancer. He had been a heavy smoker and had finally quit when the doctor diagnosed him, but it was too late. He died a year later. My brothers were little, still in elementary school, and I was only fifteen. I had to take care of my brothers because our mom fell apart when Dad died. She couldn't get a job, and we lost everything. We had to leave our home, in Portugal, and move in with my mother's Chinese-American family in the States. I was a stranger in a strange land, and I knew no one. I had to go to an American high school, far away from my friends, and I was terrified."

"I'm so sorry to hear that, Miss Torres, but why are you telling me this?"

"Because I know what you're going through, V. This is my third year of teaching here, and I work in the English department with your mom. She is an incredibly brave and inspiring woman. I just want you to know that if you ever need anyone to talk to . . . I'm here."

"No. You don't know what you're talking about, and you

don't know anything about me or my family. I'm sorry your dad died, and that you had to go through all that stuff, but you're wrong. My mom is not dying. She beat it. Her cancer is gone."

"That's wonderful to hear, and I hope it stays gone. I really do. I'm sorry. I didn't mean to upset you or overstep. I just wanted to reach out—"

"Why are you being so nice to me?"

"Because I see my younger self in you . . . walls up, angry, putting on a thick-skinned, tough façade and feeling like you're carrying the weight of the world on your shoulders. Thinking you have to be brave for your mom, for Emma and Brylee . . . for everyone. Keeping everyone else at arm's length. I get it. I was an angry girl, too."

"How did you stop being so angry all the time?" A tear slid down my face, and I wiped it away.

The bell signaling the end of break rang.

I jumped. "I have to get to my next class—"

"It's all right. I'll give you a note."

"Where are your students? Don't you have another class to teach right now?"

"No, this is my prep period. But to answer your question, I stopped being angry when I started forgiving."

"Forgiving? What do you mean? Your dad died from cancer. Who did you have to forgive?"

"Everybody. I was mad at the world. I was mad at the cigarette companies for giving my dad cancer, mad at my dad for not quitting sooner, mad at him for leaving me, mad at my mom for being so weak. The list goes on . . . and I forgave them all. But mostly, I had to forgive myself."

"I don't understand. I'm not mad at myself."

"Aren't you?"

I thought about all the counseling I had gone through last

year. Our school counselor, Dr. Sykes, said that Brylee, Emma, and I had PTSD. She wanted us to see an actual psychologist outside of school. We had to go separately because we'd all survived different traumas. We each needed specialized, one-on-one treatment.

I had fooled them all. I had told them what they wanted to hear, and they had deemed me "cured." I had tricked them into releasing me from therapy because I'd thought it was a waste of time and I didn't feel like talking about my feelings. I never wanted to talk about my feelings.

Yet, this teacher tells me I need to forgive myself and suddenly I feel the dam is about to burst. *What the heck?*

"V? Are you all right?" Miss Torres stood up and put her hand on my shoulder.

Before I could control it, rein it back in, enormous tears escaped from my eyes, slid down my cheeks, and splashed onto the desk. I put my hands up to my wet face to stop it—but the tears just kept streaming. "What's happening to me?" I wailed.

"You're releasing emotions you should have released months ago. You've been holding it all in, putting up that brave front you've gotten so good at. You've even fooled yourself. It's time to let it go."

Yes, she has kind eyes. And I think she must have some kind of magical powers, too. What is she doing to me? My thoughts were a jumble of swirly images, emotions, and memories. Nothing I wanted to talk to Miss Torres about. Yet, I felt lighter. I felt calm, and I'd stopped crying. "How old are you?"

She laughed. "How old do you think I am?"

"Ugh, I hate that question. I'm not very good at guessing people's ages. It's just that you look like you could be one of us, like a senior in high school. But you're so wise . . . and grown up and authoritative. You already have a reputation for being a strict teacher. I can't figure it out. Are you twenty-six?"

"Promise not to tell the other students?"

"I promise."

"I'm twenty-four."

"No way! But how? I mean, you had to go to college for five years, and you said this is already your third year of teaching, right?"

"Right. I graduated from high school at seventeen and dove straight into college. I grew up fast. My childhood ended when my dad died, and I had a huge chip on my shoulder. I had to prove to the world that I could handle anything."

"But you said you forgave yourself?"

"Yes, but not right away. That's why I want to help you. In telling you my story, I'm hoping that you won't make the same mistakes I made."

5

GOOD NEWS

I woke up Saturday morning to blaring music. "Good Day, Sunshine," by the Beatles, blasted from the Alexa speaker in the kitchen downstairs. I rolled over, picked up my phone, and blinked a few times to focus. "6:30 Sat, Sept 3," flashed from my screen.

"Seriously? Why can't my family sleep in on the weekends like normal people?" I shouted into my pillow. I then took the pillow, pulled it over my head, and squeezed it tight around my ears. No such luck; my pillow was a poor replacement for earplugs or noise-canceling headphones. Then my door slammed open, and Scotty zipped in.

"Oh good, you're awake!" he said in a singsong as he danced around my room.

"No, I'm not. Go away."

"Yes, you are, silly. You're talking to me." He giggled.

"I'm talking in my sleep. Now go away."

"Okay, grouchy bear! But you're going to miss out on Mommy's big surprise . . . and her special chocolate chip, banana, peanut butter pancakes!"

I sat up. "You had me at peanut butter pancakes, twerp. I'll be down in two minutes."

"Yay!" Scotty skipped down the stairs, two at a time.

I hurried into the bathroom, ran a brush through my snarled hair, threw on a baggy T-shirt over my tank top, and put on sweatpants. Then I headed downstairs and walked into the kitchen.

The scene playing out before me didn't make sense. Mom flipped pancakes at the stove, and Dad made fresh-squeezed orange juice. Fresh. Squeezed.

I rubbed my eyes. *Where's my family, and who are these people?*

"Good morning, V. So nice of you to join us," Mom said, winking. She turned down the music. "Oops, did the music wake you?"

"Whatever. I'm up now. What's going on? Scotty said you have a big surprise."

"It can wait," was all Mom said. She had a mischievous glint in her eye, and she wore a bright blue T-shirt emblazoned, "Underestimate me. That'll be fun." *Interesting. She must be in one of her take-no-prisoners, feisty moods today.* Her friends and countless adoring fans still lavished her with all kinds of gifts; they ranged from inspiring, to mushy, to funny. I think she liked the sarcastic graphic tees the best.

After my chat with Miss Torres on Wednesday, I'd made an effort to be nicer to people. Or at least hide my anger better. After Crash had plowed into my mom on his skateboard last year (and I had come close to beating him up), Dr. Sykes ordered me to go to anger management classes, together with the cognitive behavior therapy sessions.

Since I had fooled them so well in the therapy sessions, I ended up not having to go to the classes. Besides, the therapist said she didn't think that their anger management classes were right for me since they mostly comprised young, adult males who had been court mandated to attend as a consequence of their domestic violence charges. It got me out of it, but I still had unresolved anger that I didn't know what to do with. *But forgiving myself? For what? I don't know . . . I'll have to deal with this later.*

I decided not to tell my parents about my talk with Miss Torres, and I hoped Miss Torres wouldn't tell Mom. I didn't know what Mom's news was, but I had some news of my own. That Driver's Ed website, ddi.com, the one Crash told me about, looked perfect. I called them and spoke to one of their instructors. He said I could start right away. And they were the cheapest by far. I couldn't wait to share my news.

Once we were all sitting at the table and had taken a few bites of the amazing melt-in-your-mouth peanut butter pancake perfection, Mom cleared her throat and tapped her orange juice glass with the end of her fork.

I suppressed an eye roll, to the best of my ability, as my mother was well known for her embellishments, dramatic flair, and a few theatrics now and then. I sighed. *On with it, woman.*

"Attention everyone, I have an announcement to make," she declared.

"What is it, Mommy?" Scotty asked, squirming in his chair.

Dad had a slight grin but gave nothing away. He reached out and patted her non-fork-wielding hand.

"Today is Saturday, September 3rd. As you know, my fortieth birthday is tomorrow. Your dad and I are throwing a big party, and the theme is, 'Celebrating another year above ground!' But that's not my news. What makes today significant is . . ." She paused and took in a deep breath, then let it out bit by bit, as if to calm herself. Then she continued, "Today is special because a year ago today I was given that terrible diagnosis of stage four breast cancer; the diagnosis no one ever wants to hear. This is the one-year anniversary of my cancer diagnosis! Surprise! What makes that so remarkable *is* the fact that I'm still above ground. The first doctor I saw gave me less than a year to live. I proved him wrong. I beat the odds. My last cancer markers were clear, and I am officially in remission."

"Yay!" Scotty squealed. "Should we start decorating for the party, Mommy? Will there be cake? And lots of balloons?"

Mom looked at Dad.

Dad said, "Sorry, li'l man. This is a 'grownups only' party. We're having it at a restaurant, where there will be large quantities of alcohol. Your grandma is coming over to stay with you tonight."

"What?" I was incredulous. "Mom! When will you stop treating me like a little kid? I'm fifteen! I don't need Grandma to take care of me. I can watch Scotty just fine. Right, Scotty?"

"But I like it when Grandma comes over. She makes funny faces and tells goofy stories."

"Traitor," I grumbled.

"I know you are, but what am I?" Scotty asked, then he stuck out his tongue while putting his thumbs in his ears.

"Whatever, twerp."

"That's enough, V," Dad said.

I turned on him. "Dad, you never told me they said Mom only had a year to live. Don't you think I had a right to know that? That we could have lost Mom? What else aren't you guys telling me?"

"We could have lost Mommy?" Scotty asked. "What does that mean? Will she break into a trillion pieces and disappear, like the glass stars did in her story? I don't want Mommy to break!"

"Now you've done it," Dad whispered to me. He gave me the look that made me shut my mouth.

"No, honey," Mom assured Scotty. "I'm not going anywhere. I just told you; my cancer is in remission, which means there's no more cancer in my body. They got it all out with the chemotherapy, surgery, and radiation treatments. Don't you worry, sweetie. Your mama is one tough badass!"

"Ha ha, Mommy, you said a bad word." Scotty laughed and forgot his worries, quick to change subjects. "Can I have a puppy now?"

"Not this again," Dad groaned.

"But Alex's puppy is super fun to play with. She can fetch sticks and balls, and she runs around the backyard with us. Can we get one? Pleeeease? Can we?"

"Sure we can," Mom said.

My jaw dropped. "Wait, he gets a puppy? But that's not fair. You won't let me drive, but Scotty gets a pup—"

"Let me finish," Mom interrupted. "How about we get a puppy for your birthday next year, sweetie? We think you're a little too young to take care of a puppy now."

"But that's not fair!" Scotty whined. "Alex got one for his birthday this year, and he's the same age as me."

"Yes, but Alex's mommy doesn't work. We've been through this, sweetie. She's home all day and can take care of their puppy while Alex is at school. Daddy and I have full-time jobs, and you have soccer, and Daddy's coaching your team. We're not home enough to train a puppy. Puppies are a lot of work and a big responsibility. Let's talk about it again in a few months, after soccer season is over. And if you still want one then, we'll think about it."

"Okay," Scotty said. "Maybe I can have one when soccer's over?"

No one said anything for a beat. I barged into the awkward silence and said, "I have news." I thought my parents might appreciate my running interference.

"Well? Please, don't keep us in suspense," Dad said.

"I found a really cheap driver's training course that will let me start this week. It's called Dan's Driving Instruction, and they have an opening available. I can go Tuesday after school. The instructor said this class meets Mondays, Wednesdays, and Fridays after school, but since Monday is Labor Day, they're meeting Tuesday instead. He said they'll pick me up at school since they go there anyway to get the other students. He said most of his driving students are from our high school because he used to teach there."

"What do you mean by 'really cheap'?" Dad asked. "Is it legal?"

"Yes, of course! They have a professional website you can check out, Dad. They're totally legit."

"No. You can take the course in January," Mom said.

"What? But why?"

"Because you're not fifteen-and-a-half yet."

"The guy I talked to on the phone said I can start the thirty-hour classroom course and go on ride-alongs before my half birthday. He said I can't get behind the wheel until I turn fifteen-and-a-half, but at least I can get a jump start on the required classroom course."

"What good does that do?" Mom asked.

"Because, in California, we're only required to have six hours of behind-the-wheel driver training. But we have to have thirty hours of driver education. If I start now, I'll finish the classroom training early and can focus on the six hours as soon as my half birthday gets here."

"Hmm, how about Dad and I check out the website, find out the pricing, and get back to you?" Mom said.

"I already told him yes," I said.

"Did you give him any money?" Dad asked.

"No, he said I could give him a check from a parent on Tuesday."

"I bet he did," Mom said. "The nerve, booking the course with a child. Don't we have to grant permission or something?"

"I'm not a child."

"You're underage, and underage teens shouldn't be booking driver's courses without parental consent."

"I'm asking now."

"Are you? I thought you already told him you'd take the course."

"I hoped you and Dad would say yes, and I didn't want to lose the spot. He said their classes fill up quick, and he only had one spot left for the one that starts on Tuesday."

"I see," Mom said. She looked at Dad.

Dad then looked at me and asked, "What's the name of the website?"

"Yay!" I shouted. "It's ddi.com. Thank you so much!"

"We haven't said yes yet. We've only agreed to look at the website."

Just then, the doorbell rang.

"I'll get it!" Scotty said and hopped off his chair, racing to the front door. "I think it's Grandma."

He opened the door a crack and asked, "Who is it?" He peered through the crack in the door, then threw it open and almost knocked Grandma over as he rushed to hug her. "Grandma! Grandma! I'm so glad you're here."

Mom hurried to the door to help Grandma with her bag and asked, "How was your drive, Mom?"

6

THE NECKLACE

The rest of the weekend dragged along. For once, I didn't enjoy the extra day off that the Labor Day holiday provided from school. We celebrated Mom's fortieth birthday Sunday with a gourmet feast and a three-layer chocolate cake, all made by Grandma. Mom was happy, but tired. I think her 'adults only' party the night before wore her out. She took naps on Sunday and slept most of the day Monday.

Grandma and I put together a 1,000-piece jigsaw puzzle of a gorgeous red convertible sports car, the car of my dreams. We went to a craft store to pick up more yarn for Grandma's knitting habit, and I saw the picture of the car on the puzzle box. I wasn't big on puzzles, but this one I just had to put together. Lucky for me, Grandma loved puzzles. She was happy to buy it so it would give us something to do together over the weekend.

Scotty had three soccer games. Since Dad was also the team's coach, they were gone part of Sunday and all day Monday.

Grandma left Monday night, and I couldn't wait for school

on Tuesday. Okay, let me correct that: I couldn't wait to start driver's training. After some more begging and pleading, Mom and Dad finally said yes! I think they caved just to get me off their backs, but I didn't care why they said yes—I was just happy they did.

Finally, Tuesday morning arrived. I was ready. It was the first thing I'd looked forward to in a long time. I'd finally be able to start driving! My driver's training course would meet Mondays, Wednesdays, and Fridays after school until I completed the thirty-hour classroom work, as well as the six hours of behind-the-wheel instruction. Since yesterday was Labor Day, today was the only time we'd meet on a Tuesday.

I'd no sooner gotten out of my parents' car when Emma and Brylee ran up to me. *This is new.*

"V, we need to talk to you," Emma said and grabbed my arm, pulling me to walk faster.

"Have a great day, girls!" Mom said, waving.

"Hey, watch it," I said and pulled my arm back, rubbing the area she'd squeezed. "What's the hurry?"

"Sorry, but this can't wait. We need you."

"Really? *You* need *me*?" I couldn't hide my bitterness at this sudden turn of events. Where was Emma when I had needed her? I hadn't seen either of them since Brylee practically told me off while defending Crash on the first day of school. Emma had ghosted me the rest of the week. It seemed my only friend was Crash, who'd asked me about Driver's Ed every day all week. He'd even texted me over the weekend to ask if my parents had said yes.

"I'm sorry, V. Last week was hard for me, being the first week back at school," Emma said. "It brought up too many memories, so I had to go to a lot of counseling sessions. Anyway, I know I haven't been a good friend to you. I promise to be better, but right now we have to talk to you about something really important."

"What is it?" I asked.

"Someone broke into our house while we were out, and my mom's diamond necklace got stolen last night!" Brylee blurted out.

"That's terrible, but what does that have to do with me? Why are you telling me this?"

"We need you to find out who broke in so we can get the necklace back," Emma said.

"Hold on there. You want me to find a stolen diamond necklace? Are you out of your minds?"

"You found us!" Emma and Brylee said together.

"Yeah, but—um . . . well, that was different. I had to find you. Besides, I'm not a real detective, you know. I got lucky. You should call the cops and file a police report."

"We can't," Emma said.

"Why not?"

"Because Brylee's mom doesn't know it was taken," Emma said, and glanced at Brylee.

"I borrowed it without asking," Brylee admitted. "She keeps it in a safe, but I hadn't returned it yet. I hid it in my underwear drawer."

"That's the first place they look!" I said, shaking my head.

"So you'll do it? You'll take the case?" Emma asked.

"I'm sorry, but I can't help you. There's no case to take. And I'm not a cop. It's not like I can go to the scene of the crime and dust for fingerprints and then check my vast criminal database for a match. This is way out of my league. No can do. Sorry, Brylee."

"What if I think I know who took it?" Brylee asked.

"Then ask them to give it back or tell the cops. I can't help you. I want nothing to do with this. Now, if you'll excuse me, I have to get to class." I turned and walked away before either of them could talk me into getting involved.

I WALKED into Computer class just as the tardy bell rang. "You're late, Miss Jiménez," Mr. Applebottom said.

I shrugged and hurried to my seat. There was no use arguing with him.

Crash shot me a look, eyes wide and eyebrows raised. *What's his problem?* I focused on my computer screen, blocking my view of Crash. I couldn't think about him right now. All I could think about was Emma and Brylee and how they wanted me to find a stolen necklace.

Could I do it? I mean, could I really find a missing diamond necklace? My palms grew sweaty, and my pulse raced at the thought of it. *Wait a minute. Why am I even considering this? That's it, I've totally lost it now. I've officially gone crazy. There's no way I could do this again. Searching for Emma and Brylee last year got me in tons of trouble. I was in way over my head, and I saw terrible things. My parents grounded me for two months. I'm not even a real detective!* I blew out a loud, explosive breath, not realizing I'd been holding it in.

"Are you all right, Miss Jiménez?" Mr. Applebottom and half the class were looking at me.

Great. I've got to stop getting lost in my thoughts in the middle of class. "Fine, sir. Sorry."

It's true I wasn't a real detective, but I did solve a *real case*. And not just any case, but a huge kidnapping case that not even the FBI could solve. Maybe I had a special talent. I mean, Emma has soccer. Soccer is her thing.

My sixth period Dance teacher, Miss Parks, is always telling us to find our 'thing,' so maybe solving cases is my thing. It's not anything physical or athletic, that's for sure. I took Dance this year to get out of P.E. It was the least sporty thing I could find that counted as a P.E. credit, and I sucked at dance, too.

And yet, with absolutely zero training—other than watching every single episode of *Veronica Mars* over and over— I had single-handedly found Emma and Brylee, at all costs. I had succeeded where Detective Lomeli had failed. I'd solved an actual case as a real-life teenage detective.

It felt good. And I wanted to feel that rush again. Finding my missing friends gave me a purpose and made me feel alive. And it kept me from worrying about my mom. *Well, at least I don't have to worry about her anymore.* I smiled, my mind made up. *I'm going to solve the case of the stolen necklace! Now, what would Veronica do?*

A wadded-up piece of paper landed on my keyboard, knocking me out of my thoughts—again. Class was nearly over, and I hadn't paid attention to a single word Mr. Applebottom had said. I had no idea what today's assignment was.

I shook my head, silently scolding myself for not paying attention, and opened up the crumpled paper. It was a note.

> *Meet me by your locker during break.*
> *I need to talk to you.*
>
> *—Z*

Z? Did I know a Z? Oh yeah, Crash. Duh. I forgot his name was Zack because I still called him Crash. And no way did I want to talk to him right now. I needed to work out a plan for solving this necklace case. And the first thing I had to do was talk to Brylee again, without Emma. As if that was even possible. I made a mental note to stay far away from my locker during our morning break.

I PAID attention to Miss Torres in second period English, especially since she had singled me out as her pet project, thinking she could help me forgive myself or whatever. So when the break came, I wasn't ready to talk to Brylee yet. I still needed to make sure I really wanted to do this. I decided to go to the library and do some quick research first. Plus, Crash would never think of looking for me in the library.

The rest of the day progressed without incident, thankfully. I successfully avoided Crash, Emma, and Brylee. Going to a big high school and not having any classes with them (except for Computers with Crash) definitely helped. By the time the bell rang to let us out at the end of the day, I grabbed my backpack and headed out the doors with everyone else.

I realized I didn't have time to find Brylee without making me late to meet my Driver's Ed instructor. I at least wanted to make a good impression on the first day. I hurried over to the meeting spot the instructor and I had agreed to on the phone: in the visitor's parking area, first space on the right.

Sitting in the designated parking space was an old, ugly mint-green four-door Ford Fiesta. It had door dings and a dented front bumper, with "Dan's Driving Instruction" magnetic car signs on both front doors, and a yellow "student driver" sign on the roof.

"You've got to be kidding me," I said under my breath as I slowed my pace, walking toward the car.

A man wearing glasses, with sallow white skin, shaggy light brown hair and mustache, round face, and an ample belly that refused to stay within the confines of the buttons on his short-sleeved, pocket-protected, yellow shirt, climbed out of the front passenger seat to greet me. "Viola! So nice to meet you. My name is Dan Carter, and I'll be your instructor for our driver's training course. Please, call me Dan." He extended his hand, but I didn't shake it.

"And please, call me V. Besides, it's Violet, not Viola."

"Oh, sorry about that," he said, as he dropped his hand. "I'm not the best at remembering names."

"That's okay. Um, why are there others in the car? I thought it was just going to be us?"

"Oh no, you're not old enough to start the behind-the-wheel training yet, remember? This is a ride-along. Go ahead and sit in the back next to Shelly. You can watch today and learn from Zeke and Shelly's driving lessons."

Zeke? I peered through the windshield and saw Crash sitting in the driver's seat. "Um, do you mean Zack?"

"Ah yes, Zack. Of course. Do you two know each other?"

"Well, no, not really. But he did tell me about your course last week. And I think he goes by Crash."

"Hmm, does he? I'll make a note of that. Thanks for telling me where you got the referral. That's excellent! I love to hear that my students are referring me. That makes me so happy. Excellent. Simply excellent." There was a pause as he clapped his hands together and rubbed them up and down. "Welp, should we get going then? Get in the back, V. Oh, wait in the car for a bit, guys. I have to talk to someone."

I got in the car and whispered to Crash, "Hey, why didn't

you tell me you'd be here today?"

"I tried to, but you blew me off," Crash said. "This morning with that note, remember?"

"You could have sent me a text."

"When you didn't show up—to your own locker, I might add—I decided you deserved the surprise. So here I am. Surprise!"

I glared at the back of his head.

Our instructor stood next to the car, talking with a teacher from my school. The way they casually chatted, I guessed they probably knew each other. I turned to Shelly next to me and smiled. I recognized her. "Hey, didn't we have Geometry together last year?"

"Yeah, we did. Hi, V," Shelly said.

"So, what's the deal with our instructor?" I whispered. "He seems kinda weird."

"I don't know. This is my first lesson. He told me that Zack and I will take turns driving today."

"And it's my second lesson," Crash—*er, Zack* said, obviously listening in. "I started last week. But I thought he seemed a bit off, too, so I asked around. He's harmless enough, though. Some of his past students described him as 'a quirky geek trying to be cool.' He asks everyone to call him Dan, but we mostly call him Mr. C.

"Also, rumor has it that he lets kids drive before their half birthday. So you might get to drive early, V. I guess he future dates the logged hours, so it counts toward the requirements to get your permit. That way, you can be completely finished with the course before you even get your permit."

"What's the point of that? I still have to have an adult in the car with me until I'm sixteen," I said.

"True, but at least you can start driving right away instead of having to wait to get through this course first," Crash said.

"Hmm, I guess. So?" I asked.

"So what?" Crash asked back.

"Are you fifteen-and-a-half?"

"Yeah, my half birthday was August 20th. I got my permit the day before school started. Now I just have to get this class out of the way, and I'll be good to go."

"Wanna know what I heard?" Shelly piped up. Without waiting for an answer she continued, "I heard that instead of Dan's Driving Instruction, the kids call it DUI, to stand for Dan's Underage Instruction. Isn't that funny?"

We didn't laugh.

"Come on, don't you get it? Because DUI really stands for Driving Under the Influence."

Again, we just peered at her.

"Whatever. Forget it." She lowered her voice and continued in a whisper, "But I also heard he makes fake IDs."

"What?" I said. "That's terrible. If that's true, he's issuing fake driver's licenses to kids who aren't ready to drive yet. What if they get into an accident?"

"I know, it's awful," Shelly said. "But what if—"

"Okey dokey, artichokey, who's ready to go for a drive?" Mr. C got in the car, and we all froze.

7

IT'S A NICE DAY FOR A DRIVE

With Mr. C in the passenger seat, and Crash behind the wheel, Shelly and I began our first lesson at Dan's Driving Instruction. Before he let Crash put the car in reverse, he said he wanted to go over a few rules first. "The first rule of driving—or actually, just getting in the car—is what? Shelly?"

"Um, check your mirrors?" Shelly said.

"Well, yes, but before that. What's the first thing you do when you get in the car, any car? V?"

"Put on my seat belt," I answered.

"Excellent! Yes, that's correct. So, does everyone have their seat belts on?"

"Um, Mr. C?" Shelly said.

"Yes, Shelly, what is it?"

"You don't have your seat belt on."

"Oh? Ha! Well, that's because I was turned around, talking to you two. In any event, let's get going, shall we? I can talk about the rest of the rules later." He put on his seat belt and said, "Go ahead, Zeke, check your mirrors and slowly back out."

"Yes, sir," Crash said. "But my name is Zack."

"Oh yes, so it is," Mr. C said.

Crash had already adjusted the driver's seat and mirrors while Mr. C was talking with the teacher in the parking lot, but he pretended to do it again so Mr. C would see him. The car was already on and had been idling because it was ninety-seven degrees outside and we needed the AC. Crash looked left and right and over his shoulder, then put the car in reverse and slowly backed out of the parking space. He drove out of the school parking lot and turned left. "Where am I driving to, Mr. C?"

"Uh, you can call me Dan, ya know. You don't have to be so formal, Zack, or should I call you Crash? And lose the 'sir,' too, okay? My dad was sir. I'm a more casual, laid-back guy, ya know?"

"Yes, sir. Sorry, but I can't call you by your first name. That's not how I was raised. If it's okay with you, I'd rather call you Mr. C. And please, call me Zack."

"Fair enough, Zack. Fair enough." Mr. C sighed. "Well, since it's such a nice day for a drive, let's go to the Mini Mart by way of the freeway. That way, you get a little practice with on- and off-ramps."

"You got it," Crash said. He turned on his blinker and eased into the left lane to merge onto the 57 freeway, going north. Once on the freeway, he drove about sixty-five, nice and smooth, like a natural.

"Wow, Crash, I'm impressed," I said. "You're a pretty good driver."

"Thanks, V. My mom took me driving a few times before I joined Mr. C here, and today is my second lesson."

"Don't worry, V," Mr. C said. "There's not much to it. Once you get the basics down, you'll be driving like a champ someday, too."

Ten minutes later we pulled into Milo's Mini Mart, and Mr. C announced, "Okay, everyone out. Go get yourselves some slushies on me! We're taking a little break while I stay out here and make a quick phone call."

He gave Crash a ten-dollar bill, and we all got out of the car and went into the store. Once inside, we went toward the slushie machines in the back. Crash stopped by the counter to talk to the clerk. "I saw your 'hiring' sign. Could I get an application?"

"Sure, kid. But you have to be eighteen to sell alcohol. Are you eighteen?"

"No." Crash started to take the application but hesitated.

"That's okay. It just means that you won't be able to work the store alone. Some shifts, we have two or three employees here. It depends how busy it is. Go ahead and fill it out; if the boss is desperate enough, he'll hire you."

"Thanks." Crash took the application and walked toward Shelly and me at the slushie machine.

"Why do you want a job here?" I asked.

"I'm saving up to get a car. As soon as I get my license, I gotta have my own wheels."

"Oh. When will you get your license?"

"On my birthday, of course," Crash said, gawking at me. Then a wide grin slowly spread across his face, revealing dimples on both sides. "You do like me!"

My eyebrows furrowed. "What are you talking about?"

"You want to confirm when my birthday is so you can buy me a present."

"Whatever. You're such a dork."

"Who? Me? I'm hurt."

"Save it, lover boy. Let's get our slushies so you can impress me with your mad driving skills again."

"But won't it be my turn to drive next?" Shelly asked.

Crash and I shrugged, then we walked toward the check-out counter. By the time we'd all gotten our slushies there was a line.

I looked out the front window for Mr. C, and the car was gone. "Guys, look. Where's Mr. C? Here, take this." I shoved my slushie into Crash's hand and ran out the front door. The car wasn't in the parking lot. I walked around to the side of the building and saw a narrow alleyway, next to a dumpster and a fence.

Something told me to keep going. I got a tingly feeling in my stomach and tiptoed around the dumpster. On the other side, I saw the Driver's Ed car a few feet away. Mr. C sat behind the wheel, and the trunk was open. There was another car, a navy blue sedan, parked next to the back of Mr. C's car. The other car's trunk was open, too. There were two guys standing near the back of the Ford, but I couldn't see what they were doing. I shifted my position to try to make out the other car's model and license plate, but there wasn't one. I mean, nothing. It looked like the emblem and lettering had been pried off, and the license plate holder was empty. *How odd. Why would they take off the—oh my gosh! That's a stolen car!*

Suddenly, both trunks slammed shut, startling me. The two guys hopped into the mysterious blue car and sped away. Mr. C turned on the ignition and made a U-turn, heading back toward the parking lot in front of the Mini Mart. I ducked behind the dumpster until he passed me. When I walked back to the front sidewalk, Crash and Shelly were waiting with my slushie. Mr. C pulled up to the curb.

"What was that all about?" Crash asked as he handed me my drink.

"I don't know, but I'm going to find out," I said.

Mr. C got out of the car and asked, "Who wants to drive?"

"Me! I do," Shelly said.

"All right, Shelly. It's your turn. Now, is this your first time driving?"

"Yes, sir. I mean, um . . . Dan."

"There ya go! That's the ticket. Well, then. Let's all get in and buckle up. We're going to head over to an empty parking lot where I can safely teach you the basics first."

Mr. C got back in on the driver's side, Shelly got in the front passenger seat, and Crash and I had to share the back seat. "Try anything and I'll punch your lights out," I whispered.

"You say the sweetest things," Crash said, giving me a wink.

8

WHAT WILL THE NEIGHBORS SAY?

I had Mr. C drop me off a block from my house. After witnessing whatever that was with the two guys and the stolen car, I didn't trust him. Was he making fake IDs for the guys with the stolen car? I didn't think so because they looked old enough to drive. I couldn't figure it out yet, but I would. This proved he was into something illegal, so I guess Shelly was right. Whatever it was, there was no way I wanted him knowing where I lived.

We'd dropped Shelly off first—well, Mr. C let her drive herself home. She didn't do terrible, but she did ride the brakes pretty hard. I guess she did okay, considering it was her first time behind the wheel. Instead of letting Crash drive again, Mr. C got behind the wheel and said he was in a hurry. He said the driving lesson was over and he just wanted to take us home.

I hopped out of the car and waved goodbye from the sidewalk, watching them drive away before turning around and heading in the opposite direction to walk home. When I turned onto my street, Mrs. Snelling waved me over. She lived four houses down from ours and was our street's self-proclaimed

"Neighborhood Watch" expert. She knew when everyone went to work, what time they typically got home, and what they drove. She even knew which neighbors were home during the day.

"Hello, V. How are you?" Mrs. Snelling asked, taking off a gardening glove and tucking a wisp of gray hair back inside her sunhat.

"I'm good. Your roses look beautiful, as always."

"Thank you. I'm afraid the season is almost over for them. I've got a few late bloomers, but for the most part . . . oh, there I go again. You know I could talk about my garden all day. But I waved you over here because I wanted to ask you about a blue car."

That got my attention. "A blue car?"

"Yes, I saw an unmarked blue Honda parked in front of the Petersons' at noon today. It was very suspicious. You know, there's been a rash of robberies in the area, and I wondered if you'd seen anything."

Unmarked? Robberies? What?! My pulse quickened, and I got a queasy feeling in my stomach. I had to find out if the car Mrs. Snelling saw *on my own street* was the same car I saw at the Mini Mart. This was too close to home, and with Brylee's mom's necklace missing, too, I felt sure they had to be related. What the heck was Mr. C up to? I definitely intended to find out. "What do you mean by 'unmarked' car? Do you mean an undercover police car?"

"Oh, goodness no. It was obviously hot," Mrs. Snelling said as though I were an idiot. "Pardon me, I used the wrong term. I meant the car was debadged."

Now I did feel like an idiot. "Debadged?"

"Debadging is when people remove the manufacturer's emblems and logos from a vehicle that designate the make and model. Car enthusiasts and collectors do it for all kinds of reasons, but criminals do it to make the car more invisible, harder to identify. They'll boost a car, debadge it, take off the license plates and any other distinctive markings, and then use the car to commit various crimes. Once they're done with their crime spree, they'll ditch the car or burn it and move on to another one and start all over again."

"How do you know all this?"

"I watch a lot of crime and detective TV shows."

"Oh, I see. Then how do you know it was a Honda?"

"Honda Accord, actually. A 2010 model. I know because I have one just like it, only mine's Radiant Red."

I looked around.

"It's in the garage, dear."

"Of course. Wow, you sure do know your cars."

"Nonsense. People know what they're familiar with. Tell me, V, what do you know?" She looked at me hard, like she suspected me of something. Or was I just paranoid?

"I know that I better get home. My parents are expecting me for dinner soon. Thanks for letting me know about that car, Mrs. Snelling. I'll keep an eye out. See ya later." I walked away at a fast clip before she had a chance to ask me anything else.

"Goodbye, V. Be careful," she hollered behind me.

AT DINNER, Dad asked me, "How was your first day of driving school?"

"It was great," I said, mustering up my cheerful voice. I didn't want to give my parents a reason to pull me out. "I got to go on a ride-along."

"What?" Mom said, frowning. "I thought you were supposed to be doing your thirty hours of classroom instruction first. I imagined you sitting in a classroom—safe."

"Nope. Mr. C takes a more hands-on approach. Two students get to ride and observe while one student drives. He teaches us the rules of the road and safe-driving practices and then quizzes us orally by saying 'Pop Quiz.' He then asks questions in a rapid-fire round, asking a different question to each student."

"But a student-driver is driving? While you're in the car? What kind of irresponsible—?"

"Mom, it's perfectly safe. I promise. It's a training car, remember? Relax. Mr. C used to teach Driver's Ed at our school. But they had to let him go when they stopped offering that class at public high schools, so he opened up his own driving school. I'm surprised you don't remember him."

"What's his name again?" Mom furrowed her eyebrows.

Uh-oh. Now I've done it. Suppose she digs up dirt on him and exposes him for the crook he is? What if he got fired from teaching at our school because of the fake IDs? But if he got caught, wouldn't he be in jail? I can't quit now. There's a case here, and I'm going to solve it. Oh no, Mom's still waiting. I don't see a way out of this. . . . I better answer her question before she gets suspicious. I cleared my throat and said, "His name is Dan Carter, but the kids call him Mr. C."

"Oh yeah, I remember him," Dad said. "But you're mistaken, V. He didn't teach at Sierra; he taught at Orange. I met him at one of those required teacher trainings at the district office about ten years ago. Nice enough guy."

That's odd. I was sure I heard him say he taught at Sierra. Why would he lie about that? Hmm. I plastered a huge smile on my face and said, "Great! See, Mom? He's nice. Dad even thinks so. You're worried about nothing."

"Well, I guess, but . . ." Mom paused and rubbed her chin.

I saw my getaway and took it, standing up as I said, "Well, I've got a ton of homework to do. May I be excused?"

My parents nodded in unison. Homework trumped chores every time in our house. Having teachers for parents wasn't all bad, at least not when it came to getting out of dish duty and housework.

As soon as I got to my room I pulled my phone out to text Brylee. I had a feeling this was all connected somehow, and I might as well start with her.

> Hey Brylee, we need to talk.

V? You never text me. What do you want?

> Wow, I thought you wanted my help, you ungrateful little snob. I'm taking on your stupid case.

Okay, I didn't send that last one. But I wanted to. Brylee was an ungrateful snob. However, it wouldn't do any good to make her mad when I needed answers and she was the only one who could help me. Instead, I texted back,

> I've decided to take on your case and I have a few questions I need to ask about the robbery. Can we meet at school tomorrow?

Great! Thanks, V. Emma said you wouldn't let us down. Wanna meet us at lunch?

Us? I admit it, that hurt. Since when did Emma and Brylee become an 'us'? Emma was supposed to be *my* best friend, not Brylee's. Whatever, I couldn't think about that at the moment. Anyway, I had to see Brylee alone. I might get more out of her if Emma wasn't right there listening.

Sorry, no. Lunch doesn't work for me. How about we meet after school?

Perfect. Meet me at the bleachers. I'll be watching Emma's soccer practice.

Figures. Thankfully, Brylee couldn't see me roll my eyes.

Sounds good. See you tomorrow. Bye

9

TRUCE

The next day trickled by like an icicle melting one slow drip at a time. I stared at the clock in each class, willing the second hand to move faster. Drip, drip, drip. In third period, Algebra 2, I got a text from Crash that Mr. C had to postpone our driving session today, to meet half an hour later. I was relieved because I'd been so focused on talking to Brylee that I'd completely forgotten about it.

By the time the last bell rang at the end of the day, I was already sitting on the bleachers, waiting for Brylee. Miss Parks let our Dance class out early because she had an appointment to go to; it felt like my first break all day.

From where I sat, I saw Brylee before she saw me. I studied her. She was dressed in all black again, as usual. Today's outfit was a slight variation, though. She wore a black mini-skirt with a sleeveless crop top to match, and black Vans. She didn't usually show this much skin, and I couldn't help but notice how long her legs were. *Runner's legs. Hmm, why do I despise exercise so much?*

She saw me and waved, tossed her backpack over one

shoulder, and jogged over. She towered over me at five-foot-nine, to my five-foot-two. Her raven hair reached the middle of her back, those cold eyes staring menacingly at me, and her facial features had more angles than curves. But she was stunning, the kind of beauty to be admired from a safe distance. Like a raven or black panther before it goes in for the kill.

"Why are you staring at me like that?" Brylee demanded.

"What? I'm not st-staring," I stammered. "Sit down. We have to make this quick. I have to be somewhere."

"I know. You have driver's training with Crash. He told me."

"Why would he tell you that?"

"We're friends, remember?"

"Yeah, about that. How do you and Crash know each other? He's in my grade, not yours."

"Gee, thanks, genius, I didn't know that. It's none of your business. So, who's the one wasting time? Aren't you in a hurry?"

"Right, let's get to it. Let's start with the obvious first question. Who stole your mom's necklace?"

"How the hell should I know? That's what you're for, remember?"

"But you already told me you knew who took it."

"I was mistaken. I have no idea who took it. Again, that's for you to figure out."

"I can't help you if you don't tell me what you know. Do you want me to find the necklace or not?"

"Yes, of course I do. It's just that . . ."

"It's just that what?"

"He told me I was imagining things. He said everything's fine and to just leave it alone. He said he'd never do anything to hurt me. He promised me he had nothing to do with it."

"Whoa, Brylee, slow down. Who are you talking about?"

"I can't tell you. He has nothing to do with this. Just forget I said anything."

"Not likely. Tell me or I'm walking away right now and you'll never see your mom's necklace again. Is that what you want?"

Brylee looked out at the soccer field as the players walked on, heading to practice. She smiled and waved when she saw Emma.

Emma waved back.

My eyes were trained on Brylee, watching her every move, looking for a crack in her armor.

"Emma says I can trust you. But can I?" She glanced at me, and I saw something in her eyes for the first time—fear.

I met her gaze and softened my own. "Yes, you can trust me. I know you've been through a lot, and I'm so sorry for everything that happened to you when you were kidnapped, but I'm not your enemy. I'd like to be your friend, if you'll let me."

"Yeah, Emma told me that, too. She speaks very highly of you. Did you know that? It's just that, well, I don't make friends easily. Even before last year. Everyone knows my family is from Argentina and that my father is a wealthy cattle rancher there. I hear the mean things they say about me, that I'm a spoiled princess and a rich snob, stuck up, mean, cold. I hear it all. So I might as well live up to it, right?"

"What? People say that about you? That's terrible." My face reddened as I lied, guilty of thinking those same things about her myself.

"It's okay, V. You don't have to pretend. I know you don't like me."

Oops. I want her to talk to me, but I'm not prepared for this kind of candor. Okay, game on. I can be honest, too. "It's not that I don't like you, Brylee. I don't even know you, not really. What I don't like is that you took my only friend away from me. You and Emma have been inseparable since, well, since last year, and she barely talks to me anymore. I just want my best friend back."

Brylee's face hardened, and her eyebrows furrowed. Were her walls going back up? She didn't owe me anything, even though I rescued her from those monsters. What did I expect? That she'd open up to me and we'd become besties and braid each other's hair? Ha. That's a good one. Emma and I did that once when we were ten. "Don't worry about it. Let's just focus on finding your necklace, and then we can go our separate ways. Deal?"

"Give me a minute, will you?" Brylee gritted her teeth and crossed her arms, as if suddenly cold. "This isn't easy for me, okay? I'm trying. But you don't know how lucky you are. I've never had a best friend before. Actually, I've never had a friend—not a real one. Emma was the first person to befriend me without wanting something in return. She helped me through the worst experience of my life. I thought our captors were going to kill me. All the other girls stayed away from me because they singled me out so much. The others were afraid that if they were nice to me, our captors would turn on them, too. But not Emma. She stood up for me. She snuck me food when they stopped feeding me. She gave me a blanket when they stripped me of everything. And it was Emma who risked her life to wake me up when you showed up to rescue her. She could have left me there, but she didn't."

"I'm sorry . . . I didn't know."

"I don't want you to feel sorry for me. I just need you to understand that Emma is my friend, too, and I'm not giving her up."

"Of course. I had no idea, Brylee. She never told me what you guys went through, what happened to you."

"I know. I'm sure you can figure out that it's not easy for us to talk about."

"Right. So . . . about your mom's necklace?"

Brylee laughed. "Subtle, V. Real subtle. So yeah, I'm glad we had this little chat. Here's what I can tell you. When I noticed the necklace was missing, my first thought was that Santi took it. That's why I told you I thought I knew who took it. But when I asked him about it, he swore he didn't take it. He told me he'd never do anything like that."

"Santi? Am I supposed to know who Santi is?"

"Oh yeah, sorry. I keep forgetting that you and Emma are only sophomores and know nothing about this school."

"Whatever, just tell me."

"He's my boyfriend. Look, here's his picture." She took out her phone and showed me the image on her Lock Screen. It was of Brylee with her arms around a good looking guy with short, black hair and brown skin.

"He's cute." I nodded encouragingly and gave her back her phone.

She took the phone back, looking at it and smiling before continuing. "So Santiago—Santi—is a junior and new this year. He said he had to leave his old school in Santa Ana because the local gang was pressuring him to join up. He transferred to our school to get away from the bad crowd there."

"Whoa, seriously? A gang?"

"You really don't know anything, do you?"

"I do, too," I protested. "I've heard of a gang called the Pico 7."

"Okay, impress me. What do you know about them?"

"They're based in Santa Ana."

"Duh, I just told you that." Brylee shook her head.

"Fine, I don't know anything," I admitted. "What does this have to do with your mom's necklace?"

"Only that I'm telling you Santi didn't take it. When I asked him about it, he got mad at first and said I didn't trust him. But then he was sad; he admitted he almost gave into the pressure and joined the gang. He said if he didn't transfer schools and get out of that area fast, something bad would happen. He said the gang's leader is a scary dude with a thirst for power. He recently took over when their other leader was killed in a knife fight with a rival gang called La Palma 91. They're having turf wars or something, and Santi had to leave before either gang recruited him. The Pico 7 gang terrorizes Santi's old school and neighborhood in Santa Ana, and the La Palma 91 gang runs Anaheim. That's it. That's all I know."

"Does Santi drive a dark blue Honda Accord?"

"What? That's random. No, he doesn't. Why would you ask me that? He doesn't even have a car. He takes a city bus to school every day."

"Never mind. It was just a hunch. What else can you tell me?"

"Santi doesn't like to talk about it. He said it's in the past and he wants to focus on his future. He only told me anything at all because I asked him about my mom's necklace. He says he wants to stay out of trouble, graduate from high school, go to college, and do something good with his life. I believe him because he has a good heart."

"Then why did you think he took the necklace?"

"I was afraid he might have been forced to steal it by the new leader."

"But you said he wasn't in the gang. And that he told you about them *after* you accused him."

"Don't turn this around on me. He told me a little about the bad crowd at his old school when we met, before we started dating. I'd also heard things, enough to worry about him. But he told me not to worry. He said he'd never do anything to hurt me."

"So you don't know anything about the other robberies in the area then?"

"Have there been other robberies?"

I nodded.

"No, I had no idea."

"Okay, thanks. I better get to my driving lesson. And Brylee?"

"Yeah?"

"I'm glad we had this talk."

10

LOST AND FOUND

I showed up to our meeting spot in the visitor's parking lot, but no one was there yet. I pulled out my phone and looked at the clock on it. I was five minutes early. *Good, maybe I can digest everything Brylee just told me. I can't imagine the horrifying things that she must have endured during her kidnapping. All this time I've tried so hard not to let my mind go there. . . .*

Just then, Mr. C pulled up into the empty parking space in front of me. *Well, so much for thinking about it now.* He got out of his car and said, "Well, hello there, V. Aren't we punctual? Hey, would you mind helping me get the car ready? You can put the magnetic signs on the doors while I put the student driver sign on the roof. Okay?"

"Sure, Mr. C."

"Super. Uh, let me just get the trunk open." Mr. C went to the back of the car and opened up his trunk. He brought out the yellow roof sign and fiddled with it while walking toward me. "Well, don't just stand there; I've got to mount this, and this little part is loose. Go get the door signs."

"Okay, okay." I peered in the trunk at the two rectangular

magnet signs. The rest of the trunk looked empty, except for a wadded-up cargo net in the back corner. I don't know what I expected to see, but I felt disappointed. Yesterday, the trunk looked full of backpacks and trash bags.

I pulled out the first sign, took it to the driver's side, and stuck it on the front door. I went back for the second sign and grabbed at it, but my hand slipped off and brushed up against the cargo net. Something sparkly within the net caught my eye. I leaned in for further inspection and thought I saw diamonds. *What the—?*

I poked my head out and saw Mr. C was still fiddling with the roof sign. I leaned back in, reached to the back of the trunk, and brought out the cargo net. A stunning diamond necklace was tangled up in the netting. There must have been at least forty diamonds on that thing. *Whoa! Could this be Brylee's mom's necklace?* I couldn't believe it. I worked it loose as fast as I could and shoved it into my sweatshirt pocket.

I grabbed the other sign, took it out, and walked around to the passenger side to put it on the car.

"We all set here?" Mr. C asked.

"Yes, sir."

"Sir? Didn't we go over this yesterday?" He laughed. "Wow, the royal treatment, huh?"

I just stared at him.

"Um, are you all right, V? You look a little pale."

"Yeah, I'm okay, Mr. C. But I just realized I forgot about my counseling appointment. That Dr. Sykes is a stickler for punctuality, ya know."

"Who? Why would I know that?"

"Because you said you taught here before. I assumed you knew the school psychologist."

"No, I don't recall saying that. I told you kids I used to teach at Orange High, your rivals."

Hmm, this is interesting. He's changing his story already. Oh crap, does he suspect I'm onto him? "Oh, my bad. Well, sorry, but I have to go. Dr. Sykes really is strict. See you Friday." Heart racing, one hand over the lump in my sweatshirt pocket, I turned around and ran back to the school. I texted Brylee with trembling fingers as soon as I rounded a corner, safely out of Mr. C's sight.

> Where are you? I need to see you NOW.

> Bleachers. Still. Watching Emma's soccer practice. Duh.

I jogged over to the soccer field and quickened my pace when I saw Brylee stand up from the bleachers. She put her hands on her hips and glared at me.

As I approached her, I got a side cramp. Wincing and out of breath, I motioned for her to follow me under the bleachers.

"Run much?" Brylee mocked. "What's with the mystery stuff? Emma said you were a bit dramatic, but come on. Even for you, this seems a little overkill."

I waited until she followed me under the bleachers and stopped talking. It gave me a chance to take a couple deep breaths to steady my nerves. I closed my eyes. When I opened them, Brylee stood directly in front of me with her arms folded, staring at me with bewilderment.

"You won't think I'm so crazy when you see this," I said, reaching into my sweatshirt pocket. I pulled out the necklace. "Recognize this?"

"Oh my god, where did you find that? That's my mom's necklace!" She cupped her hands together and held them out, as if begging me to give it to her. I was surprised she didn't just snatch the necklace from my hand; I figured it must be super valuable. I dropped the necklace into her outstretched, cupped hands.

"Be careful!" Brylee warned. "These diamonds are worth thousands of dollars, probably more than you could earn in five years."

"Obviously, since I don't actually have a job right now and I earn, uh, exactly zero dollars." I rolled my eyes. "If this necklace is so expensive, then why on Earth did you steal it from your mom in the first place?"

"I didn't steal it. I only borrowed it. Santi took me to a fancy restaurant, and I wanted to look nice for him. Besides, I planned on returning it to her safe as soon as I got home."

"Why didn't you?"

"She was at a fundraiser that night, so I thought I had plenty of time, but she came home early and went straight to her room. I didn't get a chance to—wait a minute. Why am I explaining myself to you? Where did you find this?"

"That's the thanks I get?"

"Thank you, V," Brylee said through pursed lips. "Now, where did you find it?"

"You won't believe me."

"Try me."

"In the trunk of my Driver's Ed teacher's car."

"I don't believe you."

"Told you."

"Seriously? That doesn't make any sense. How did it get in there?"

"I'm trying to figure that out. I think this case is bigger than just your mom's necklace, but you can't say anything to anyone, especially Santi—okay?"

"Why? He'll be happy I'm not getting grounded. Mom doesn't even know it was missing. This is awesome! I could almost hug you . . . almost. I'm going to go home and put it back in her safe right now. Tell Emma I said to—"

"Brylee, wait. You can't tell Santi. Promise me you won't tell him, okay?"

"But why not?"

"I think my Driver's Ed teacher and that gang are involved in the robberies. I saw a couple guys putting stuff in his car yesterday, and I think this necklace must have slipped out of one of their bags. If you tell Santi, he might tell the gang. And that would be bad for us."

"Don't be silly. Santi doesn't even talk to them. He wants nothing to do with them. If anything, he'd be pissed that stupid gang robbed my house."

"Brylee, I know you don't want to think the worst of him, but what if Santi really was the one who took it? He had access, he saw the necklace, and he knew where you hid it. He could have easily swiped it if he was alone in your room for a second. Please, just give me a week to figure this out, okay? Please."

Brylee's eyes opened wide as she stared at me. It was like I could see the tiny lightbulb finally go off behind her enlarged pupils as she made the connections, realizing I could be right. She looked down at the necklace and ran her finger along each of the sparkly gems, thinking. "Oh no!" she gasped.

"SHH! Brylee, what's wrong with you? Someone will hear you."

She held the necklace up and pointed at it, too shocked to speak.

I knelt down and squinted at it. Near the clasp at the back, two of the smaller gems were missing. The empty pear-shaped facets looked naked among the forty or so large diamonds surrounding them. "Uh-oh. . . . Well, it's in the back, so maybe your mom won't notice. How often does she wear this, anyway?"

"Hardly ever, which is why I borrowed it in the first place. But if she does notice, she'll know I borrowed it without asking . . . and she'll kill me."

II

SANTIAGO

Brylee offered to drive me home, but I wanted to walk. I needed to clear my head. I had to figure out what kind of a scheme Mr. C was running. I couldn't make any sense out of it. Mr. C definitely didn't seem like the type to run a burglary ring, especially one that involved a local gang.

He seemed like a nice enough guy. He was a bit quirky and tried too hard to be 'cool' with the kids, but he was harmless. *Wasn't he?* He also seemed soft and dopey, sort of spineless. Definitely not a leader of any kind, especially organized crime. It just didn't add up. If this gang really was working for him, he sure did have a great cover act. I guess I had to give him credit for that.

A block from my house I spotted a dark blue car parked on the street. It looked like the same car I had seen at the Mini Mart the day before. *Could it be?* I approached the car, and sure enough, it had been debadged, just like Mrs. Snelling described. The license plates had also been taken off. *This has to be the same car. So, if this car is here, that means there's a robbery taking place somewhere nearby. Hmm, I wonder . . . could the burglar be stupid enough to be robbing this house with the getaway car out front in broad daylight?*

I looked up at the house in question. I couldn't be sure, but I had a feeling. I peeked in the passenger window, which was rolled down, and saw the car key still in the ignition. *Seriously? Man, this is way too easy.* I reached in through the window and pulled out the key.

I heard a door open. I ran around to the other side of the fence in the front yard and ducked down behind it. I peeked over the top edge just in time to see a guy who looked like the picture Brylee had shown me of her boyfriend. Santiago (or Santi, as Brylee mentioned everyone called him) walked around the house from the backyard, carrying a large duffel bag. Then he ran past me and jumped into the car. After a few seconds, a thunderous racket emanated from the car with a high volume of curse words and expletives.

Santi jumped back out of the car and searched his pockets, swearing the whole time.

I stood up from my hiding spot and walked out to the sidewalk, near the car. "Are you looking for this?" I held the car key up for him to see. "What are you doing, Santi? Are you the one robbing the neighborhood? I know you stole a diamond necklace. What else have you taken?"

"You don't know shit! How the hell do you know who I am? How'd you get the—oh never mind. Just be a good girl and give me back that key."

"I've seen your picture. You wouldn't want your girlfriend, *Brylee*, to know about this now, would you?"

Santi's face scrunched up, and he closed his eyes. For a second there I thought he was going to cry. He found his voice and glared at me, "Girl, you do not want to mess with me. This is way over your head. Now, give me the key. I'm not gonna ask you again."

"You haven't asked yet. Tell you what, I'll trade you this key for what you've got in that bag in your front passenger seat."

"You're loca, chica," Santi sneered. "No deal. And if I don't get back with this stuff right now, they're gonna mess me up."

"By they, you mean the Pico 7?"

His eyes narrowed, and he balled up a fist. "Listen, chica, you better shut up and mind your own business."

"If you don't tell me what I need to know, I'm gonna mess you up."

"Yeah, right. What do you weigh? I bet my Chihuahua weighs more than you." He looked me up and down and crossed his arms. "You and what army?"

"I don't have to resort to violence to hurt you; I'll just tell Brylee about our little meet-up today." I walked to his car and opened the passenger door. I set the bag on the floor mat and got in, straddling the bag.

"Crazy bitch," Santi muttered. He got in the car and grabbed the steering wheel with both hands, squeezing hard. His knuckles turned white as he stared ahead. "What do you want?"

"Let's go for a ride and have a nice chat," I said, all smiles, handing him the car key.

Santi grabbed the key and shoved it in the ignition. He turned the key, started the car, floored the gas pedal, and peeled out, all in one fluid motion. We sped through the residential streets of my neighborhood as I put on my seat belt and wondered if this was such a good idea.

We stopped at a red light. I exhaled, and realized I'd been holding my breath. I finally broke the silence with, "Tell me about your leader. Is he forcing you to steal?"

Santi let out a long sigh. "Yeah, he is. But please, you can't tell Brylee. If she finds out, she'll leave me; she's the only good thing I have. You've got to understand, I never wanted any of this. I didn't ask to join this stupid gang. I've been trying to keep my nose clean. That's why I transferred to your school. And then I met Brylee, and she dug me, ya know? She made me think I could actually turn my life around, finish high school and graduate, and like, have a life, ya know?"

"You can," I encouraged, not sure what else to say. I didn't expect him to open up so easily and was a little taken aback.

"Nah. You don't know Pedro, man."

"Who is Pedro?"

"Wow, you really don't know nothin', do you?" He paused. "You know what, screw it. Honestly, it feels kinda good to get this off my chest, to be able to tell someone. Even if it is a little white girl."

I winced but stayed silent.

"Okay, so Pedro is the new leader of the Pico 7. He and the guys jumped me last week. They put a pillowcase over my head and took turns kicking me while the others held me down. Then Pedro, he gets real close and whips off the pillowcase. He says he wants me to read his lips so I understand him real clear, and then he says, 'If you don't join up, you leave me no choice but to kill you myself . . . mi hermano.'" Santi shook his head and sniffed, holding back a sob.

"Wait, is Pedro your brother? I don't understand."

"Yes, he is. Now are you going to let me finish telling you this or not?"

"Of course. Sorry. Please continue."

"So that stupid necklace was my first score. My initiation. It was an easy steal. I figured Brylee's mom was insured, ya know? I didn't think she'd get so freaked out about it. But once I took it, I couldn't give it back because I'd already turned it over to Pedro. Besides, it's gone now. It's too late."

"No, it isn't. I found the necklace and gave it back to Brylee today."

"You did what? How is that possible?"

"Later. First, you answer my questions, then I'll answer yours."

"Fine. What else do you want to know? I don't know how I can help you. This is my life now. There's no way out. But I'm just not ready to lose Brylee. Please. Not yet."

"That's not true. There is a way out. There's always a way. And I can help you."

"You? Don't be so naive. How could a little thing like you possibly help me?"

"Again, I don't need brute force. I have a brain, and I know how to use it."

Santi laughed. "Whatever. I'm not as dumb as you think, ya know."

I smiled. "I know. I'm counting on it. Tell you what, you're going to help me catch the gang and stop these burglaries. They'll go to prison for a long time, and you'll be safe. You can get your life back, Santi. But first, you have to tell me about your real leader. The guy your brother reports to."

"Don't call him that. I despise him and hate that we're related. I don't need reminding. But you're wrong. There is no 'real' leader. Pedro reports to no one. He took over as gang leader a couple months ago when their other leader was killed in a knife fight against Diego."

"Who's Diego?"

"He's the leader of La Palma 91. Anyway, Pedro has been in a gang since he was fourteen, since our dad died six years ago. Now Pedro's twenty and power hungry."

"I'm so sorry. How did your dad die?"

"In a gang fight."

"Oh . . . I, uh . . ."

"Save it. I know what you're thinking, and I don't want your pity. What else do you want to know?"

"What about Mr. C? How does he fit into all this?"

"Mr. who?"

"Santi, if you're protecting him—"

"No, I'm not. I'm telling you the truth. I can't believe it, but I am. I'm desperate enough to put my faith in a skinny little white girl, dios mío. I've got to get away from this life, because if I don't, I'm afraid I ain't gonna be in this world much longer."

"So you're telling me that you don't know who Mr. C is? Mr. Dan Carter?"

"Oh, Dan? You mean Dan?"

"Um, I guess so, yeah. He asked us to call him Dan, but we all call him Mr. C. He's my Driver's Ed teacher, and I know he's involved. I saw two guys putting stuff in the back of his car yesterday."

"That was you?"

"What are you talking about?"

"The two guys were me and Chewy. Chewy thought he saw a girl by the dumpsters, and I told him he wishes. But there really was a girl? And it was you? Ha ha! That's funny."

"Not to me. I thought I kept out of sight better than that." I looked out the window, chastising myself for nearly getting caught. "So what is Dan's role if he's not your leader?"

"Chica, you got it all wrong. Driver Dan isn't the one in charge. He's just a pawn, like me. Pedro's blackmailing him to work with us."

"What? That doesn't make sense. Why would he blackmail a middle-aged driving instructor? How do they even know each other? And . . . stop calling me white girl and chica. My name is V. Also, my dad is from Costa Rica."

"Well hello, V. It took ya long enough to introduce yourself." Santi chuckled and continued, "Yeah, Pedro said he's gonna kill Dan's wife and kids if he doesn't cooperate and do what he's told."

"I didn't know he had kids . . . or that he was even married. But threats to kill them? Isn't that extortion?"

"I don't know about that. Whatever. I don't care. Do you want to hear this or not?"

"Of course I do. What else ya got? Please, tell me everything."

"Driver Dan and his wife are separated because their kid is really sick. I guess that can put a strain on a marriage. Anyway, Dan lives with his mom now, and Pedro pays him to help us so he can pay the kid's hospital bills."

"Oh my gosh, that's terrible."

"That ain't the half of it."

"How did Dan get mixed up with Pedro's gang?"

"Now that's a great story, and I'd love to tell you, but first, you gotta promise me something."

"What's that?"

"You gotta promise me you won't tell Brylee about any of this. She's the best thing to ever happen to me."

"If you help me catch these guys, including catching your brother—um, sorry, I mean Pedro, I won't tell her. You have my word."

"Okay, chica—I mean, V, settle in. It's story time. But first, I gotta make a delivery."

Santi pulled into the parking lot of a rundown strip mall. He leaned toward me, and I flinched. "Chill, I'm just gettin' my bag. Be right back." He reached down by my feet, grabbed the duffel bag, and ran off toward a cigar shop.

I had no idea where we were. He'd been driving through city streets, never taking the freeway the whole time we'd been talking. I didn't pay attention to any of the street signs. I got out of the car to have a look around, but before I could go anywhere, Santi came running back and said, "V, get back in the car! We gotta get out of here—now!"

I sped back to the car and jumped in. "Where are we?"

"Some place you don't wanna be, girl. I shouldn't have brought you here, but you didn't leave me much of a choice now, did you?"

I shrugged.

"It's okay. I'll take you home now, and along the way I'll tell you a nice story, the story of how Pedro and Driver Dan met. Buckle up!"

I put my seat belt on.

Santi backed out of the strip mall parking lot and spun the car around, then made a right turn out of the exit without stopping. He began his story in an animated tone. For the first time that afternoon, he seemed happy and carefree.

"About a month ago, Pedro, Javi, and Chewy set out to rob an old lady's house. They'd been watching it, and they knew she wasn't home. The only problem? Her son, Dan, was."

12

DRIVER DAN

Santi continued, "It was about eleven at night and the house was dark, not even a porch light or streetlight outside. That's one of the reasons Pedro picked it—easy to get in and out of, no lights, no security, no dogs. But he thought the old lady lived alone; he didn't count on anyone being there. . . ."

As I listened to Santi tell me the whole story, I imagined it from Mr. C's perspective. I could picture him in my mind. . . .

★ ★ ★ ★ ★

DAN CARTER HEARD a crash and a window breaking, just as he slipped into bed. Startled, he eased out of bed, trying not to make a sound. His heart raced as he grabbed a golf club out of the closet, the first thing he could find. He tiptoed barefoot down the hall, clad in baby blue pajamas with purple hearts and teddy bears on them—a gift from his six-year-old daughter. He'd only moved into his mother's house four days ago. The separation from his wife a fresh wound, he pined for his family. The PJs, as obnoxious as they were, brought him comfort, and he wore them every night. He longed for reconciliation, but he just didn't know if his wife would ever take him back.

He stopped midstep when he saw a shadow on the wall above the hallway night-light. He thought it might be his imagination playing tricks on him, and he scolded himself for leaving his glasses on the nightstand. He flicked on the hall light, only to be confronted by a short guy (Chewy), wearing a bandana over his head, and holding a gun. Said gun was pointed directly at him. *I'm a dead man.* His thoughts turned macabre as he wondered if his family would have to identify his bullet-riddled, bloody body with the stained teddy bear PJs at the morgue.

"Hey, guapo, somebody's home," the short guy said. He looked at Dan and laughed. "What are you gonna do with that golf club, teddy bear boy? I don't see no balls around here. You sure ain't got any."

A much bigger guy (Javi) ran up the stairs and said, "Shut up, Chewy. Get the club." Both guys rushed Dan and pinned him against the wall while Chewy wrestled the golf club out of his hands.

A third man (Pedro) took his time walking up the stairs. He sauntered down the hall toward Dan and the two guys holding him down. He stopped, a mere inch from Dan's face. He closed the distance another half an inch until they were almost touching noses. He sneered and said, "Give me a reason not to kill you right now, teddy bear boy."

"Hey, that's what I called him," Chewy said, laughing.

Javi stifled a laugh, trying not to smile.

"I got nothing," Dan said. "My wife and I just separated. I got a sick kid in the hospital. I lost my job. I'm trying to get started up with a new—hell, just do it. It's not worth living anyway. Go ahead and kill me. I'm worth more dead than alive, and I've got nothing to live for. Take whatever you want. There's not much here."

"Ya know what? You're right," Pedro sneered. "There's not much here. You're pathetic. Do you know how pathetic you are?"

"I know. I'm very pathetic. I'm done. You'd be doing me a favor by just killing me now."

"Yeah, man, is that right? 'Cuz I don't do nobody favors."

Chewy let go of Dan and whispered something in Pedro's ear.

The leader walked into Dan's bedroom and looked out the window. "Hey? That your car?"

"Yes," Dan whispered. "The keys are there on the nightstand. Go ahead and take them and go." He closed his eyes, silently pleading.

"Driver Education, huh?" the leader said. "I didn't take no Driver Ed. Chewy, did you take Driver Ed?"

"Nah, boss. You taught me how to drive, remember?" Chewy said.

"Oh yeah, that's right, cuz. We didn't have no fancy Driver Ed teacher teachin' us. We did it the D-I-Y way."

"That's a good one, boss," Chewy said.

"Silence," the leader said. "I'm thinking." He paced a couple times around the room while the others watched. Then he walked back over to Dan and said, "Ya know what? I don't do nobody favors. So today's your lucky day, my friend. I'm not going to kill you. But . . . you will do me a favor. Let me tell you how this works. You're gonna drive to a designated location, and I'm gonna put something in your trunk. You're gonna get a paper with an address, and drive there. No questions asked.

When you get there, you stay in the car and pop the trunk. My boys on the other side will retrieve the cargo and leave an envelope. You are not to look at them, talk to them, or look in the trunk until you're back home, alone. Understood?"

Dan gaped at him.

"I will do this at my leisure, when I want to. You will be at my beck and call. Do you understand?"

"No, I don't understand."

"Well then, let me spell it out for you, dumbass. You are going to be my errand boy. You are going to be a transporter for me and my boys. In exchange, I will spare you your life. You know I can come back to this house any time I want—and slit your throat."

Dan gulped.

"And, since you've told me you value your life so little, I'm going to need insurance. Chewy, get me his wallet. Where is it, teddy bear boy?"

"It's next to my keys on the nightstand," Dan said.

Chewy walked into Dan's room. He turned on the light and picked up the wallet from the nightstand. He walked back and handed it to the leader. "Here ya go, boss."

The boss took the wallet and opened it up, flipping through it, and pocketing the cash. "Aw, what a cute family you have here, Dracul Edmond Carter." He took out Dan's driver's license and read his home address out loud. "Hmm, I think I know where that is. If not, I'll find it easily enough. But clearly, that's not where we are now, is it, Dracul?"

"This is my mother's house. I'm just staying here temporarily. And, please, it's Dan. Call me Dan."

"I don't think you're in a position to be making demands, Dracul. But then again, with a name like Dracul, I'm gonna cut you some slack. From now on, I'm gonna call you Driver Dan.

You're gonna drive where I tell you, when I tell you, and I'll pay you for your time. As long as you do what I say, your family stays safe and you make money to pay off the sick kid's bills. See? I'm a nice guy. This is a win-win-win! Right, boys?"

"Right, Pedro!" Javi, the muscle-bound giant said.

"Javi, how many times I gotta tell you not to say my name in front of people, huh?"

"But we said Chewy's name. And just now, you said mine . . . so I figured it was okay."

"Oh, you figured, huh? Well, it doesn't matter anyway, because now Driver Dan is our amigo. He's not gonna tell nobody nothin'. Isn't that right, Driver Dan?"

Dan nodded.

"This is good. We begin tomorrow. Be at Milo's at two o'clock."

"Milo's?" Dan asked.

"Do not interrupt me, estúpido. Milo's Mini Mart. Look it up. Now, listen carefully. I hate repeating myself. You will do exactly what I say." Pedro stopped talking and got in Dan's face, uncomfortably close.

Dan gulped and began sweating but forced himself not to look away. Finally, he broke the silence with, "I'm listening."

"Good. It's about time. So, as I was saying, make sure you park on the east side by the alley. The back of your car will face the entrance to the alleyway. Roll down your passenger window, put your hands on the dash and your head on the wheel. Do not move. If I were you, I'd close my eyes, too. When you hear the trunk close, the paper with the address on it will be sitting on your passenger seat. Got it?"

"But what if I have my driver's training students in the car?"

"What? I gotta think for you, too? Send 'em into the store to buy some candy. That's on you, bro. Just make sure you're alone in the car when we come by, or we'll keep on drivin'. And trust me, you do not want us to keep driving."

"AND SO IT BEGAN. That's how Driver Dan became a transporter for the Pico 7 gang," Santi finished, just as he pulled up to my house to drop me off.

13
VISITING LOMELI

The school buzzed about the sudden rash of break-ins in the area. Apparently, our neighborhood had been deemed highly "break-in-able." I walked around my own block last night, trying to figure out why this area had been targeted. It was a cloudy, moonless night, so dark I could barely see my hand five inches in front of my face. And then it hit me.

The streets were dark. Too dark. Most of the streetlights weren't working, and many of the homes didn't have their porch lights on. Also, since we lived in the Old Town District of Orange, our homes were preserved by the historical society. Most of them had been built in the early 1900s, which made them some kind of historical treasure or something. To me, they were just old. But old houses meant no modern home security systems, alarms, or cameras. Some people didn't even bother to lock their doors. Everyone always felt safe here—or, at least we used to.

I couldn't be sure, but I had a feeling the recent increase in crime had to do with Pedro and his gang, especially after hearing Santi's story of how they had robbed and threatened my Driver's Ed teacher. And of course, Santi's gang initiation. But why were they so stupid? I mean, I caught Santi robbing a house in broad daylight yesterday. That's not just bold; it's downright stupid.

There had to be more going on here than just Santi's initiation. There were too many break-ins, and there's no way Santi was involved in all of them. *Hmm, it could be that since Pedro is the gang's new leader, he feels he has to prove himself to the rival gangs . . . or something like that?*

The more I thought, the more confused I became. Every thought led to more questions. I needed real, concrete answers, not just my own theories. But who could I ask? It's not like I could just walk into the police station and make them tell me what they knew about the break-ins.

Wait a minute. Of course I could. I just had a brilliant idea! School could not get out quick enough for me to put my plan into action, yet it was only fourth period. *Ugh.*

"V? Pssst, V."

"What?" I turned around and glared at Kevin, my Chem Lab partner.

"Where were you just now? Were you sleeping with your eyes open again?"

"Yeah, something like that. I've got a lot on my mind. So what do you want?"

"Do you have any lead I can borrow? I just ran out."

"I don't use mechanical pencils."

"Well, then, do you have an extra pencil?"

"I think so. Hold on." I rummaged through my backpack until I found a pencil. I handed it to Kevin. "Here ya go."

"Thanks. I'll give it back when the bell rings."

"Don't bother. You can keep it. I found it in the trash, under a bunch of half-chewed hamburger meat."

"Gross. I'm not touching that." Kevin was vegan.

"Relax, dude. I'm just messing with you. Here, take the pencil already."

When the lunch bell rang, I couldn't get out of there fast enough. I didn't feel like dealing with anyone, especially Crash who'd already badgered me this morning in Computers about missing my driving lesson yesterday. And I couldn't face Brylee yet, now that I knew about her boyfriend's involvement with his brother's gang. No, I had to leave campus and get some answers. It was time to pay a visit to my old pal, Detective Lomeli.

I HAD to sneak off campus since only the upperclassmen were allowed to leave at lunchtime. I half jogged, half walked to the police station, a little less than a mile away. Once inside, I took a deep breath, collected my thoughts, then channeled my nerves and tried to look panicked. *It's showtime!*

I walked up to the front desk and scrunched my eyebrows together, frowning. Two uniformed police officers were in the area, but no one paid attention to me. I cleared my throat.

Nothing.

"Excuse me, I need to report a robbery," I said, in my best high-pitched, 'I'm really scared' voice.

Bingo. That got their attention. Both officers rushed to the desk. "Are you all right, miss? Was anyone hurt?"

"Well, no. I mean, yes, I'm all right. No one was hurt."

"When did this robbery take place?"

"Well, actually, could I speak to Detective Andrew Lomeli? I'd feel more comfortable talking to him, if it's okay."

The two officers exchanged a look. The first one shrugged. "Cool, less paperwork for me." She turned to leave and added, "Hold on, miss. I'll see if he's available."

The second officer went back to his desk, sorting through files, happy to ignore me again.

I wandered around the small waiting area, hoping I'd caught Lomeli on a good day.

"V?"

I turned around and saw Lomeli standing with his arms crossed.

"You want to report a robbery, but you can only talk to me? Hmm, and this is something that can't wait, I suppose. I should be asking you why you aren't in school right now."

"It's nice to see you, too, Detective."

"Uh-huh. Now tell me, why do I feel like I'm going to regret this little impromptu visit?" Lomeli sighed. "Come on back. Let's catch up in my office, shall we?"

"Ooh, an office. You're moving up in the world."

"Can it," Lomeli said as he closed the door and pointed to the chair in front of his desk. "What brings you in here today, V? And don't tell me it's because of a robbery."

I wandered over to a bookshelf instead of the chair Lomeli wanted me to sit in. "Nice office." I picked up a framed photo of a young, attractive black man in a police uniform. "I didn't know you had children. Who's this hand-some young man?"

"Thanks. I don't. My nephew. Anything else?"

"Yeah, is this a police academy photo?"

"Graduation. His name is Alan, he's too old for you, and he has a girlfriend anyway. Why are you here, V?"

"He just graduated? Wow, you must be so proud. I bet you already got him a job here, too."

"I am, and I did. Now put the picture down and stay out of my family business. For the sake of repeating myself, why are you here, V?"

I finally perched on the edge of the chair. "Actually, sir, I'm concerned about the robberies in the neighborhood."

Lomeli sat on the corner of his desk and crossed his arms again, glaring down at me. "I see. And were you robbed?"

"No, but Mrs. Snelling told me about some robberies on my street."

"Oh no you don't, young lady. Didn't you learn anything last year? Don't go poking your nose around where it doesn't belong." He shifted and stood up. "For your peace of mind, if by 'robberies' you mean the break-ins, then technically, they're 'burglaries.' So far, no one was home and no one was hurt or threatened in these petty thefts, and nothing of great value has been reported stolen. Therefore, it's not a robbery. Now let us do our job, V. You can rest assured we're on top of it."

"That's what I want to talk to you about."

"Oh?"

"I know the Pico 7 gang is involved."

A vein throbbed in his temple. "If you need to know anything about the Pico 7 gang, it's that they're dangerous. All the more reason for you to stay out of it. You're just a kid. Why can't you be a normal teenage girl and stay out of trouble? Go back to school and finish your afternoon classes. After school, you can go shopping at the mall with your friends, or get your nails done, or whatever it is teen girls do these days."

"I don't have any friends."

Lomeli just stared at me. He walked over to the window, his back to me, then began tapping his foot. Finally, he said, "Okay,

I'll take the bait. What happened between you and Emma? I thought she was supposed to be your BFF for life, right? Isn't that why you risked your own life, disobeyed my orders to stay out of it, and tracked her down last year?"

"Yeah, and if I hadn't found her, she'd be dead by now."

Bingo. That sent him over the edge. He began pacing around, trying to control his temper. "V, you know that's not true. You botched up a major FBI criminal investigation, remember? They were closing in on the other factions to shut down the entire operation, not just—wait a minute. I know what you're doing. You think you can outsmart me, missy?"

"Why, Detective, I have no idea what you're talking about."

He walked back to his desk in two large strides and moved a legal pad to cover the files resting there. "We're through here, V. I suggest you leave before I arrest you for truancy."

I gasped and put my hand over my mouth. "You wouldn't."

"Try me."

I put my hands up in 'surrender' and stood up. "I'm going. I'm going. It was good to see you again, Lomeli. We'll have to do this more often."

"I'd rather not."

"I'm hurt. Well, have a nice day. Bye." I turned the knob on the door and opened it without looking back or bothering to close it again. I had what I came for. I'd be a little late to AP Euro, but it was worth it.

14
THUNDERBIRD

About twenty-seven hours later, I was back at the Mini Mart with Crash and Shelly after Shelly had nearly killed us driving here. It was my second lesson (since I'd bailed Wednesday), but it was Shelly's third behind-the-wheel day, and I figured she'd be a better driver by now.

Still, I was grateful for the ride-along because I got to observe Mr. C without his noticing. While he was busy giving Shelly guidance and taking over for her when she took both hands off the wheel to cover her eyes, I peppered him with questions.

"Mr. C, are you married?"

"Yes, V, I am. Why do you ask? Shelly, slow down."

"Because you're wearing a wedding ring, but you never talk about your family. Do you have a family? Like, kids?"

"Shelly, you're following too close. You need to back off a bit. Easy. No, don't slam on the brakes. Just ease up on the gas. There ya go, good. . . . Um, yes, V. I have three children."

"Well, where are they?"

"They're at home, with their moth—Shelly, no! Don't take your hands off the wheel!"

"I'm sorry, Mr. C," Shelly wailed. "I couldn't help it. I thought that truck was going to hit us. It was a reflex."

"We'll have to work on your reflexes, Shelly. It's okay, kids. We're all okay." He let out a rush of air, as if he'd been holding his breath.

When we reached the Mini Mart, everyone was ready to get out of the car and kiss the ground.

So there we were. Santi's story checked out so far. Mr. C had confirmed everything I'd asked. Now I just needed to get a better view of Mr. C's exchange with the Pico 7 gang. Thanks to Lomeli's predictable looking out the window, pacing, and ranting, I was able to snap some pics of the open file and papers on his desk. Relief swept over me that it was the exact file I was looking for. Luckily, I wouldn't have to break into Lomeli's office later after all.

According to the file, there were two rival gangs in this area. The Pico 7 gang ran Santa Ana, and the La Palma 91 gang ran Anaheim. Our city of Orange bordered both suburbs, sort of stuck in the middle. Since Pico 7's leader recently died (murdered by Diego, La Palma 91's leader) and Pedro took over as Pico 7's new leader, a turf war broke out as both gangs competed to claim Orange so they could expand their territories. The turf war explained the recent crime wave in our neighborhood, but now I wondered if both gangs were responsible for all the break-ins.

Still, what kind of competition was that? Which gang could rob the most houses? It didn't make sense. There had to be more to it. Then again, I didn't know anything about gangs and their 'inner workings.' I was in over my head and admitted to myself that I'd have to talk to Santi again.

Once inside the Mini Mart, I ditched Shelly and Crash and snuck back outside. I headed over to the alley and hid behind the dumpsters again. I peeked over and saw another car parked behind Mr. C's, just like last time. Both trunks were open, and a guy was loading up Mr. C's trunk. But it was a different car this time. Instead of a blue Honda, it was a light gray Toyota. I could tell because it still bore the Toyota "T" emblem on the front grille.

I peered around the dumpster to get a better look at the front of the car. No license plate. I looked back at the guy loading Mr. C's car. It wasn't Santi. He wore a bandana over his head, and I couldn't see his face, but he was too short to be Santi.

"What ya doin', li'l girl? How 'bout you mind your own business and scoot."

I turned around to find a Hispanic man standing behind me. He had a pencil-thin mustache, tattoos on his neck, and a frightening coldness to his dark eyes. I gulped as I realized I must be face-to-face with the leader of the Pico 7 gang, Pedro. He matched the description in the police file perfectly, down to the mustache and neck tattoos.

I involuntarily backed up a step and smacked into a dumpster, whacking my elbow. "Ouch!" I yelped.

Ignoring my cry of pain, Pedro stepped up to within an inch of my face, staring me down. He didn't utter a word. His menacing glare bore into my soul, and the only sound I heard was my own ragged breath. I was afraid to move, afraid to swallow as I felt the saliva collect in my mouth.

Pedro reached up and touched my cheek with his left hand. "You have a pretty face, girl. I'd hate to see anything happen to such a pretty face just because you were snooping around the wrong place at the wrong time."

I tried not to flinch as he tucked a lock of hair behind my ear. I focused on the tattoo between his thumb and forefinger—three black dots like points of a triangle. *Breathe. Just breathe.*

"V? Are you down there? Are you okay?" It was Crash. He called down the alleyway but I couldn't see him.

"Say nothing about this if you know what's good for you," Pedro hissed. "Answer your friend, but don't let him come down here." He lowered his hand but didn't back away.

I swallowed hard and dug my fingernails into my palms to calm myself down. I took a deep breath and hollered, "Yeah, I'm okay, Crash. Just stubbed my toe on a rock. I'll be right there."

"Okay," Crash hollered back. "But where are you?"

"You better run. Your boy is calling." Pedro stepped back and to the side, gesturing for me to pass through the narrow opening.

I squeezed past him, bumping into him in my haste. He let out a sinister laugh, reminding me of a cartoon villain. Beads of sweat formed on my forehead, upper lip, and hands as I sprinted up the alley with everything I had. I ran toward the front of the Mini Mart, glancing over my shoulder as I ran. Pedro was gone—like, he just vanished.

"Where were you?" Crash asked when he saw me round the corner of the store's front. "And where's the car . . . and Mr. C?"

"Why, Crash, if I didn't know better, I'd think you were worried about me."

"Nah, that's just your overactive imagination acting up again. If you don't want to tell me what you were up to just now, it's cool. But can I ask one question?"

"I guess."

"What did you do with Mr. C, and more importantly, our ride home?"

Just then Mr. C pulled up and rolled down his window. "All

aboard, children. I had to run a quick errand. Sorry if I worried you. I thought I'd be back before you came out of the store. I was across the street, depositing a check at my bank."

"Who has the overactive imagination?" I said with a smirk, reaching for the car's back door handle and silently praying as I willed my racing heart to slow down.

AT TWO O'CLOCK in the morning, I heard a loud crash that sounded like glass breaking. I had been drifting in and out of sleep, tossing and turning. Bad dreams can do that to a person. I had dreamed that Pedro held a knife to my throat and threatened to kill my family if I didn't do what he said. I shook my head to get rid of the nightmare and wake up. Then I heard something else. Something heartbreaking. This time, I knew I wasn't dreaming.

"Mommy! Mommy! He's gone! He's gone! The bad men took him! Mommmmy!" Scotty screamed, crying.

Mom, Dad, and I rushed into Scotty's room at once. Clearly, everyone was awake. This was not a dream. Mom and Dad had robes on. I did not. I stood there in a tank top and underwear, wondering if I should cover up or if I should even care. I mean, this was my family. What was there to be embarrassed about?

I shook my head again, mad at myself for caring what I was wearing in that moment. I tried to focus on Scotty, on the scene in front of me. *Am I sleepwalking? Am I in shock? What is going on?*

Mom turned on the light. Scotty sat upright in bed, sobbing and clutching his covers.

"What happened, sweetie? Who's gone?" Mom soothed as she rushed to Scotty's bedside, cradling him in her arms.

"Thunderbird. They took my Thunderbird!" Scotty wailed.

Mom and Dad exchanged an uneasy look while the knowledge of what had just happened donned on them. Someone had been here. In Scotty's room. In the middle of the night. Dad ran out of the room and bolted for the stairs, taking them three at a time.

Scotty slept with his special stuffed animal every night, without fail. Ever since Mom made up a silly story when we were on a ski trip in Oregon two years ago, Scotty had been obsessed with Thunderbird. I thought Mom really did make up the whole story, but apparently Thunderbird was a well-known legend among many Native American tribes.

Thunderbird also happened to be the mascot of the University of British Columbia. A few months ago, a Canadian friend of Mom's sent Scotty a stuffed-animal toy of their Thunderbird mascot when Mom had told her about his obsession for all things Thunderbird. He had slept with it every night since. It was not a silly story at all to Scotty. He believed every word of it.

While Mom consoled Scotty, I glanced around his room to see if anything else was missing. But this didn't feel like a random burglary. Nothing else was out of place. I had a sinking feeling this was personal.

"Hannah, you'd better get down here," Dad called up. "Leave the kids upstairs."

"V, stay with your brother. I'll be right back," Mom said,

hesitating before letting go of Scotty. She got up and went downstairs to see what Dad had discovered.

I needed to see, too. My 'sinking feeling' was more like nagging guilt. I knew this was because of me. "Hey, Scotty, are you thirsty? Do you want me to get you some fizzy water?" Carbonated, sparkling water was a treat. He wasn't allowed to have it very often, but he loved it. Strange kid.

"Mm-hmm," he said, still clinging to his covers.

"Okay, champ. Sit tight. I'll be right back." I headed to the door, about to go downstairs.

"V? What if the bad guys come back?"

I stopped cold, then spun around. "Did you see the bad guys?"

"Mm-hmm."

My heart thudded in my ears, and I felt sick to my stomach. "What did you see?"

"Well, I guess I didn't really *see* them. I mean, I kept my eyes closed so they'd think I was still asleep. But I heard them. They were whispering and arguing. One of them pulled Thunderbird out from under my arm. I didn't move because I was afraid. I let them take him!" Scotty began to cry again.

"Scotty, it's okay. You did the right thing. It was very smart of you to pretend to be asleep. You are so brave and so smart. Don't think for a minute this is your fault. We'll get Thunderbird back, I promise. I'm going to get you that fizzy water now."

I crept downstairs as quietly as I could to see if I could listen to Mom and Dad without them noticing. The kitchen light was on, and Mom and Dad stood by the kitchen table, looking down at something. I felt a draft and saw that the window above the sink was broken, with glass shards around the sink, counter, and floor.

"We know you're there, V," Mom said. "You might as well see this. After all, it's addressed to you."

A chill went down my spine. I walked over to Mom and Dad, then knelt down to pick up the object they seemed riveted on, not even lifting their eyes to look up at me.

"Don't touch it," Dad said. "The police are on their way. We need to leave the scene untouched so they can dust for fingerprints."

"Carlos, you watch too many spy movies," Mom said, letting out a giggle.

"How you can laugh at a time like this, Hannah, makes me love you even more. But, darling, now is not the time."

My parents. Our lives are in danger, and they're flirting with each other like they're still dating. Ew. It's obnoxious. I rolled my eyes and studied the object—making sure not to touch it.

The only good news was that the burglars returned Scotty's Thunderbird. However, the stuffed toy was duct taped to a brick. That must have been the crash we heard, them throwing the brick through the kitchen window. But that wasn't all. Thunderbird's wardrobe had been . . . added to. It was wearing my white bra and a pair of men's socks. A giant "V" was emblazoned onto its beak in dark red lipstick, my mom's signature color.

15

SLEEPLESS NIGHT

I paled as I realized what it all meant. It was clearly a message meant for me. I wanted to scream. I knew I couldn't say anything to the police about it, or to my parents. That would just make it worse. No, this was my burden to bear. This was my fault. My family was in danger, and I felt completely powerless.

The doorbell rang. Mom sighed and got up to answer the door. Before I had time to think or plan what I would say, or even to cover myself up, two uniformed police officers barged in and asked me to sit at the kitchen table. Dad tossed me a throw blanket from the couch, and I wrapped myself up in it. He nodded reassuringly, so I went with the police to the kitchen. The two officers peppered me with questions as a third officer approached Mom and Dad.

Why did the perpetrators write "V" on the bird's beak? Did I know the people who broke into our house? Was this a prank? What was my involvement? Did I have enemies at school? Why did they dress the bird in my bra? Was there a hidden message? What was the message? Did they want to scare me? Was I scared? What did I know about this? Was it a jealous boyfriend? Why did he have my bra? Was I a good student? Did I party? And on and on.

The third officer asked my parents similar questions about their "delinquent" daughter. Scotty crept downstairs and sat in Mom's lap, curling himself into a tiny ball. All I wanted to do was go back to my room, hide under the covers, and sleep for a week. I wanted to make it all go away. Why did Pedro have to catch me spying on them? *I'm such an idiot.*

"Miss Jiménez, do you need me to repeat the question?" the first officer asked.

"Huh? What? I'm sorry. I'm just really tired. I've already told you everything I know, which is basically nothing. Can I go back to sleep now? Please?"

"I'd like to be excused, too," Mom said. "I need to put my son to bed; he's exhausted."

"Of course, ma'am, go on ahead," the second officer said. "You can go, too, V. We know where to find you should we have any further questions."

"Yes, officer, of course . . . um, thank you," I managed. I scooted my chair out and hurried upstairs before anyone changed their mind.

It was 3:47 a.m. when I finally walked into my room. Mom had just put Scotty back to bed. She reminded me I could sleep in as long as I wanted since it was Saturday. I saw the concern etched into her face. She could tell I knew more than I let on, but she didn't push. She hugged me good night and left me to my thoughts. I heard Dad close the front door downstairs. The police had finally left.

I flicked the light switch on and surveyed my room. Nothing seemed out of place. Yet, to my horror and mortification, Pedro and his gang had stolen my stupid training bra out of my dresser drawer *while I slept* and I hadn't heard a thing. I shuddered at the thought of them in my room, going through my things. My eyes flicked to the dresser. A piece of paper I didn't recognize lay next to a tube of lipstick that wasn't mine.

I walked over and picked up the note. Scrawled in the same dark red lipstick were the words,

Mind ur own biznis

I felt violated and guilty all at once. If it weren't for my snooping around, none of this would have happened. If it weren't for me, Scotty wouldn't have had to cry himself back to sleep every hour for the rest of the night, afraid the monsters would visit his room again.

Pedro's message to me was crystal clear. He took something from every member of my family. He showed me he could break in and walk around my house in the middle of the night, and enter my parents' room, Scotty's room, and mine—while we slept. He took Dad's socks, Mom's lipstick, Scotty's stuffed bird, and my bra . . . to show me how easy it was for him. I was sure he wanted to show me how he could have—just as easily —slit our throats instead.

Sleep evaded me. I stared at the ceiling, thinking of all the ways Pedro could kill me and no one would ever know. Or worse, Pedro would kill my family and leave me alive to suffer . . . or force me to watch. I shuddered again.

I remembered the tattoo I'd seen on Pedro's hand. I did a quick Google search for "3 dots tattoo" and found this:

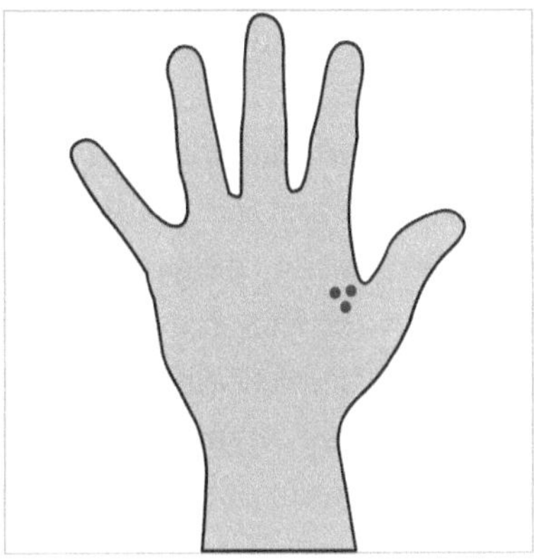

A small tattoo of 3 dots in a triangular formation is the symbol for la vida loca. The crazy life.

THE DOTS MEAN: 1. End up in hospital 2. prison or 3. dead.

I SHUDDERED. This case wasn't worth dying for and I certainly didn't want to live "la vida loca." I had to remind myself that I was just an average teenager, and not really a private investigator. I was definitely *not* Veronica Mars, my idol. I also had to remind myself that even Veronica Mars herself wasn't real. Nope, she was just a made-up, fictional character about a teenage detective on one of the best TV series ever. And me? I was a lonely fifteen-year-old with an overactive imagination.

Solving Emma's and Brylee's kidnapping cases last year was sheer luck. *And even those had nearly gotten me killed!* I had to face facts and stop acting like I was an invincible loner who didn't need anyone. I missed being normal. I missed my friends. I missed Emma.

I formed a new plan, one that wouldn't get me or my family killed. 'Operation Keep My Nose Clean' would go into effect as soon as I got a couple hours of sleep and was able to form coherent thoughts again. I decided to take Pedro's advice and mind my own business.

As sweet sleep enveloped me in its cozy blanket, I thought of Mr. C and his fake IDs; was he really being blackmailed? Santi; did he really want out of the gang? Pedro and his gang; they were criminals, but were they hard-cold killers? The secret transfers between the car trunks; a mystery I couldn't solve? I couldn't care about any of that anymore. It didn't matter. Whatever they were up to, it was none of my business.

I had a new plan. And my new plan didn't include getting killed. I needed to drop the case (that no one even knew I was working on except Pedro), and when I woke up later today, I would call Mr. C and drop out of his Driver's Ed class. Then I'd call Brylee and Emma. I had an idea that just might work to get my friends back . . . and I could enjoy my life again. Besides, I'd already found Brylee's necklace, and that's all she'd ever asked me to do anyway. Therefore, as far as I was concerned—case closed.

16

SUZIE'S RESCUE

I showered and dressed, then hurried downstairs, eager to put my new plan into motion. It was nine o'clock Saturday morning. Judging by the looks on my family's faces and that they were still in their pajamas, I assessed that none of us got much sleep last night. I guessed I got maybe three hours. I grabbed a banana out of the fruit bowl on the kitchen island, smiled and waved at my family, and headed toward the garage to my awaiting bicycle.

"And where do you think you're going, young lady?" Mom asked.

"I thought I'd go for a bike ride," I said. "It's such a beautiful morning. I'm hoping to stop by Emma's to see if she wants to join me."

At this, Mom's eyebrows shot up. "Oh? Are you two friends again?"

"Mom, we never stopped being friends. She just has a lot going on with soccer, and all her counseling appointments, and you know, healing. But she's better now, and it's time I start acting like a good friend. I really want to try harder to be there for her."

"V, I think that's great. But why the sudden change?"

"Perhaps a middle-of-the-night break-in sort of made me shift my priorities."

"Good, I'm glad you brought that up. Have a seat, V. We want to talk to you about last night," Dad said.

"They took Thunderbird!" Scotty wailed and started crying all over again.

"Carlos, not now," Mom scolded. She shifted in her seat, soothing Scotty. "It's okay, sweetie. They gave him back, remember? The nice policemen borrowed him for a few days. They need Thunderbird to help them with their case. They're going to get him all cleaned up and bring him back to you very soon."

"The bad guys wouldn't have come in my room at all if I had a dog to protect me! And Thunderbird wouldn't have to go away. When can we get a puppy, Mommy? When?"

Mom and Dad exchanged a look, and Mom went into her teacher mode as she explained to Scotty, once again, why we couldn't get a puppy right now. "Scotty, dogs are an awfully big responsibility. You have to feed them and take them outside to go potty constantly. You also need to play with them, exercise them, and take them on lots of walks. They have to be trained and brushed and groomed, and you have to give them frequent baths. Are you sure you're ready to take all that on?"

"I can do it! I can already do all those things for myself. Well, except the going potty outside part."

"Oh, really? Gee, Scotty, when do you cook for yourself?" I butted in.

Scotty looked down and mumbled, "I can make a peanut butter and jelly sandwich."

"V, I got this," Mom warned. She turned back to Scotty and

said, "Of course you can, sweetie. But that's just it; you're still learning how to take care of yourself. Taking care of another living thing takes a lot of maturity and—"

"What's maturity?"

"Maturity means things like being responsible, behaving, and acting like a big boy. Taking care of a puppy is a lot of work. You can't forget to feed it or not take it out because you're too tired or don't feel like it. I just don't think you're ready."

"But you'll help me, right? Alex says his whole family takes care of their puppy."

"That's a good point, kiddo," Dad said. "If we get a puppy, it will affect our whole family. We'll all have to pitch in and help you take care of it."

"Yay! We're getting a puppy!"

"Wait a minute. We haven't said yes yet," Mom said. "What makes you so sure?"

"Because Daddy said you'll all help me take care of it." Scotty's smile spread clear across his face.

That smile melted all our hearts. I could see Mom and Dad softening, about to cave in. A better idea popped into my head, and suddenly, I knew what I had to do.

SUZIE DENTON WAS two years older than me, and a senior. She was brilliant at science and wanted to be a chemist. She also had a passion for all things furry. At last count, I think she had one rabbit, two guinea pigs, a couple aquariums of colorful, tropical fish, and an old, three-legged stray cat who had shown up on her doorstep two years ago.

I met Suzie last year when she had helped me spy on her

neighbor, Mrs. Lee, to get information about Emma's kidnappers. Well, "helped" wasn't quite right. The truth was, she almost blew our cover. Ah, but that's a story for another time.

This year, Suzie was an office aide fourth period. I saw her in the office sometimes because I still had to check in with Dr. Sykes now and then. Anyway, I was pretty sure she'd want to help me get Scotty a puppy. After all, this was her thing. It's what she lived for—helping animals find good homes.

Suzie volunteered with OC Pom Rescue as a foster mom. Her family had fallen in love with a Pomeranian they met at a friend's house, and the next thing you know, they signed up to be a foster family for rescue dogs who needed veterinary care, training, or just a safe place to stay while waiting for their forever families. If she didn't have the right dog for Scotty, she'd most likely know how to help us find the right one. I just needed to call her.

But first things first. Once I received Mom and Dad's blessing—which was easier than I thought, even though I promised to pitch in—I was ready to put my new plan into action. Mission number one, 'Get Scotty A Dog And Get My Friends Back,' was my top priority. Forget Pedro and his stupid gang. My family and friends were much more important than trying to play teen detective and possibly getting everyone I care about killed in the process. This new plan gave me a renewed sense of hope. I took a deep breath and picked up my phone. I started to call Brylee and thought better of it, deciding to text her instead.

> Hey Brylee, do you have a car?

I saw the three dots pop up instantly. Then they disappeared.

I sent another text.

> Duh, I'm stupid. Of course I know you have a car. I meant to ask if you could pick me up and give me a ride somewhere. It's a surprise for my little brother. Are you free today?

I wanted to appeal to Brylee's sense of family loyalty. Emma told me Brylee had three younger siblings and often had to babysit them. I remembered because it struck me as odd that their names all began with a C: Cory, Catalina, and Camila. So why didn't Brylee have a C name, too? Anyway, it worked. She said she'd be at my place in fifteen minutes. Then another text from her.

> Is it all right if Emma tags along?

As if she had to ask. My plan was working brilliantly . . . so far. Now that I had the wheels and the excuse to hang out with Brylee and Emma, it was time to call Suzie.

Suzie answered her phone on the first ring. "V? You haven't called me in a year. Please don't ask me to stalk another neighbor again. My heart still hasn't recovered from the last spy mission."

"Ha ha. Okay, I guess I deserved that. So . . . hi Suzie, how are you?"

"What's up, V?"

"Um, I have something to ask you."

"Oh? What's that? Never mind. Look, can it wait? I don't have time to talk right now. I'm getting ready for a big special adoption event at the Lazy Dog, and I don't want to be late."

"Excellent! You just answered my first question."

"What question? What are you talking about?"

"Do you have any puppies available for adoption?"

"Seriously? Yes, we do! This is great! You're finally ready for a dog?"

"Yep. Actually, I want to get a puppy for my broth—"

"Wait a minute. Are you sure your parents are on board with this?"

"Yes, of course. But the dog is mostly for my brother. He's been begging us to get one, and my parents finally caved in. They said I could get one from you today. But do you only have Pomeranians? They seem kind of small."

"No, we have Pom mixes, too. Occasionally, we get in terriers. Why?"

"Scotty's only seven. I'm afraid he might be too rough with a Pom. I was hoping for something a little sturdier."

"Yeah, I see your point. We don't usually recommend Poms for families with little kids. Hmm, let me think." Suzie paused. "Oh! I know! I have the perfect pup for you! He's a mix. He just came in last week, and I'm fostering him. You can come by and meet him tonight when I get home if you want—"

"What does he look like?"

"Here, let me snap a pic. Wait a sec. Come here, boy. There."

"Got it?"

"Awww, he's so cute! Scotty will love him! Can I come get him right now?"

Suzie laughed. "Relax. That's not how it works. We have protocols in place; so no, you can't. Besides, I really have to get going. How about you come over tonight with your family for a meet 'n greet?"

"Can you just bring the pup to your event and I can pick him up there? I really want to surprise Scotty with him."

"We don't recommend surprises. What if it's not a good fit?"

"But you don't understand. Someone broke into our house last night and took Scotty's special stuffed animal. He's a worrier as it is, and now he's begging for a dog so he'll feel safer at night, and—"

"Oh no! That's terrible! I am so sorry that happened to you. Well . . . we usually do a one-week trial anyway, so I guess it might . . ."

"Please!" I begged. Suzie was many things, but a rule breaker was not one of them. It took a bit more convincing, but she finally agreed to bring the puppy to her adoption event for me to pick up there. She said she had to run it by Jas first, but as long as Suzie vouched for me, Jas should approve it.

I said bye to Suzie, promising to get a dog carrier and some supplies first. I told her we'd meet her at the Lazy Dog restaurant in an hour or so to get the puppy. I ended the call and tucked my phone back in my pocket, feeling confident that my plan was going well so far. I jogged downstairs and found Mom in the kitchen. I told her Suzie had the perfect puppy for us. Scotty walked in just then, so all she could do was give me a thumbs-up and a big smile. That was all the reassurance I needed.

I beamed back at her, tousling Scotty's hair on my way out.

"Stop it, V," he said as he squirmed away, giving me a light kick in the shins.

"Is that a soccer move?" I teased. "What kind of big sister would I be if I didn't harass you once in a while, huh?"

Scotty shrugged and asked Mom for a cookie. I took that as my cue to leave, so I grabbed my purse, shoved my feet into my Converse sneakers, and headed to the front door.

Dad stood with his arms crossed in front of the door, blocking my path.

"Dad, Brylee and Emma are going to be here any minute. I don't—"

"They can wait," he interrupted.

Oh, please don't ask me about the break-in again. I don't want to do this right now. I couldn't meet his gaze. I looked out the window by the door to see if Brylee was here yet and felt my dad take my right hand.

He turned my hand over and pressed something into my palm, then closed my fingers around it. "Here, honey. This is to help with the you-know-what. This is a great thing you're doing for your brother; he's lucky to have you for a big sister."

I opened my hand and peeked at the stack of bills, tens and twenties, then shook my head. "I don't want any money, Dad. I need to do this myself. I feel responsible for what happened and . . ."

"I know you do, sweetheart. But by the time you get all the food and supplies that come with puppy ownership, it'll cost more than you have. Just let me help you, okay?"

"Thanks, Dad," I mouthed, half-smiling. I stuffed the wad of cash in my jeans pocket, then threw my arms around him and held on tight.

He took a step back before returning the hug. "This is a nice surprise. Do I have to pay you for hugs these days?"

"Hey, that's not fair. I hug you," I said, pulling away.

Dad furrowed his brows. "Let's just say it's been a while."

"Oh. Sorry. I've had a lot on my mind lately. I'll do better."

One quick blast of a car horn startled me. I jumped.

"A little jumpy, are we?" Dad asked, grinning.

"Just excited. Well, my ride's here. I gotta go. Love you." I bolted for the door and shut it behind me before he could utter another word.

I CLIMBED into the back seat of Brylee's gray-brown Audi A6. The seats were a soft, dark gray leather, and the car was spotless. I knew Brylee's family was rich, but this couldn't be her car . . . could it?

"Hi Brylee! Hi Emma! Thanks for picking me up on such short notice like this. Scotty's going to flip when we surprise him with a new puppy."

"A puppy?" Emma said as she and Brylee exchanged a look.

"Wow, V," Brylee said. "You told me it was a surprise for your brother, but you didn't mention a puppy. What gives? Spill it."

"It's kind of a long story . . . and I'm not sure where to start." I fidgeted. "Is this your mom's car? It's beautiful, and the leather is so soft."

"No way she'd be caught driving this. As far as she's concerned, it's not a car unless it's a Mercedes. My stepdad bought me this car for my sixteenth birthday. He said an Audi wasn't as showy as a Mercedes or a BMW; he thought it would make a suitable first car for a teenager."

"Oh." I felt stupid. Obviously, rich was an understatement.

"By the way, I know what you did there, V," Brylee said. "Nice try. Now tell us why you're getting Scotty a puppy."

I let out a long sigh. I wasn't sure how much to tell them, considering I was pretty sure Santi was with Pedro when he broke into my house last night. You know, the same Santi who also happens to be Brylee's boyfriend. Oh, and of course there's that little matter that she doesn't know he's in a gang.

I wanted to tell them everything. I wanted Brylee to like me. And more than anything, I wanted my best friend back. No, I *needed* Emma back. I missed her so much. *Baby steps. Ease into it.*

I began with, "Scotty's been bugging our parents for a new puppy for a while. His best friend Alex has one, and he just won't let it go. Mom and Dad kept saying no, but he wore them down. Since my friend Suzie volunteers at a dog rescue, I told Mom that Suzie would help me find the perfect puppy. Then, when I called Suzie, she said she had one right now and that I could just come pick him up. It's a little sooner than Mom and Dad were prepared for, but it seems like it's meant to be, you know? So I called you to help me go get the dog so we can come back and surprise my brother with it."

"Hmm," Emma said. "That's not a long story. Why do I get the feeling you left out the most important part? V, what aren't you telling us?"

I looked up and met Emma's eyes in the rearview mirror. They were encouraging and probing, and I was reminded she still knew me better than anyone. *There she is.* I could never keep a secret from Emma. My eyes silently pleaded with her to let it go—for now. She seemed to understand and looked away.

We pulled into the PetSmart parking lot as I let the unanswered question hang in the air. I put my hand on the door handle and bolted out of the car as soon as Brylee put it in park. I shrugged and said, "Come on, we have to get the supplies first."

ONCE INSIDE THE STORE, we made our way to the dog section. I took out my phone and looked at the list Suzie texted me, down to the exact brand of puppy food her foster pup was already eating.

"What do you need to get?" Brylee asked. "Maybe we can split up and get the stuff so we can get the puppy sooner. I have places to be."

"Got a hot date with Santi?" Emma teased.

"Something like that. Can we go now? Please?"

I cringed at the mention of Santi's name, realizing I hadn't finished my long story yet. I didn't have the heart to tell Brylee about her boyfriend, plus I'd promised Santi I wouldn't tell. I really had no idea if he was part of the break-in last night.

I told Emma and Brylee what I needed, then I grabbed a bag of puppy kibble and two metal bowls and placed them in the cart. Emma went searching for a dog kennel, Brylee headed toward the dog beds, and I went looking for chew toys and training treats.

When we got all the supplies on the list, I said, "Let's go get Scotty's puppy! Who's with me?"

"I am!" Emma said. "I'm so excited! I just love puppies!"

"Whatever. Let's go," Brylee replied.

No one said anything on the way to the restaurant, which was fine with me because it meant I didn't have to tell Brylee about the break-in yet. That was a conversation I was not looking forward to.

"There it is," I blurted. "Brylee, Lazy Dog is on the left. You're gonna pass it."

"I know what I'm doing, V. I'm not blind. I'm going up to the light first. It's easier to go in that way. Besides, you don't even know how to drive yet, so shut up."

I did what I was told.

We pulled into the parking lot, and I saw a black pop-up tent with "OC Pom Rescue" emblazoned across it in front of the restaurant. I suddenly realized I was just as excited as my brother about having a new puppy. I couldn't wait to meet the little guy. "Come on, guys. Scotty's puppy is waiting!"

Emma squealed. Brylee rolled her eyes, but then she winked and nudged me. "It's pretty cool of you to do this for your little brother, V, whatever your mysterious reasons may be."

"Thanks, Brylee. I'm not trying to be mysterious. I'll tell you why later, I promise." Apparently, she hadn't forgotten that I hadn't finished my story earlier after all.

We walked up to the dog rescue's table and saw Suzie talking to some people, so we decided to look around. Emma saw a play pen with small dogs, mostly Poms, and jumped in with them. "Puppies!" she screamed. She sat down on the ground, and four little dogs climbed all over her, wagging their tails with glee.

"What a child," Brylee said, shaking her head. "Oh, what the heck." She reached over the pen and picked up a cream-colored Pomeranian. It licked her face in greeting. I glanced over at a nearby volunteer, and she nodded, smiling, so I got in the pen with Emma.

"They're soooo cute!" Emma cried out, then she made a face, scrunching up her nose. "Except for the licking my teeth part, I love them all and want to take them home with me."

Brylee and I laughed, then she said, "If I could have a dog, I'd want this one." She nuzzled the cute fluff ball in her arms. "Which one is Scotty's?"

I looked around at the dogs and puppies in the pen with Emma and me, then at the two other pens near us. None of the dogs matched the photo Suzie sent me. "Hmm, I don't know. I don't see him."

"There you are, V. Catch any more kidnappers lately?" Suzie said as she sauntered over to us with a wriggly puppy in her arms.

Emma and Brylee froze, turning pale, as though all the blood had drained out of them in an instant. I awkwardly shook my head and put my finger to my lips.

"Oh my gosh, I'm such an idiot!" Suzie said. "I'm so sorry. That was really insensitive of me. Clearly, I've lost my mind. Let's start over, okay? Hi everyone! V, would you like to meet your brother's new puppy?"

"Definitely!" I climbed out of the play pen and gingerly lifted the puppy out of Suzie's arms. "Oh, he's perfect! He looks even better in person. Do you know how old he is? What is he mixed with?"

"We think he's a five-month-old Yoranian."

"A what?"

"A Yoranian," Suzie repeated. "It's a Yorkshire Terrier and a Pomeranian mix, also known as a Yorkie Pom. But his mom was a Pom mix, too. We don't know her history. Thus, the floppy ears. He's very sturdy and gets along great with kids. We think he'll be about twelve pounds, fully grown."

"That's not very big," I said.

"How big does he need to be? He'll be a great dog for your brother."

I held the puppy out in front of me, face-to-face, to get a

good look at him. He licked my nose. "Do you know anything about him?"

"He had a home, but his owners had to give him up because they're moving out of the country. They were upset and said he's a really good puppy. He's even almost potty-trained. I've been working with him this past week, as much as I could."

"That's so sad that his family couldn't take him with them."

"Yeah, it is. People surrender their pets for all kinds of reasons. You'd be surprised. That's too bad for them, but it looks like you're getting a great dog here, V."

Emma skipped over and took the puppy from me. "Aren't you just the cutest thing ever!" she cooed. "He looks kinda like Benji."

"Who's Benji?" Brylee asked. She put down the dog she'd been holding and walked over to us. It seemed she and Emma had recovered from Suzie's blunder.

"*Benji* is an old film series my mom and I watched," Emma said. "Grandma saved all her old VHS tapes with movies from the '70s and '80s. They're hilarious. Anyway, Benji was a stray mutt with gold, tan, and brown fur, just like this guy. In the movies, he was really smart; he always rescued kids and stuff."

"Maybe Scotty and I should watch one of those movies. Do you think he'll want to name the dog Benji?"

"Maybe," Suzie said. "It's a cute name."

"What was the name his other owners gave him?"

"Tucker."

"Tucker?" Emma said, still holding the puppy. "What kind of a name is Tucker?"

"Talking about names already, huh?" A volunteer with a black T-shirt that said "OC Pom" on it walked up to us. She smiled at me and said, "You must be V. Suzie's told me a lot about you."

"Yes, I'm V. Nice to meet you?"

"Oh!" Suzie said, blushing. "V, this is Jas. She runs this rescue, and she's the one who signs off on whether you get to take Benji, or whatever name you decide on, home with you today."

I laughed nervously.

"It's okay, V. My bark is worse than my bite," Jas said, and winked at me. "I just have a few questions for you, and some paperwork to fill out. Normally, we'd want your parents to be here with you, but Suzie's vouching for you, so we'll make an exception this one time. Let's go over to the table and get the forms."

I walked away with Jas and looked over my shoulder as Emma called out, "Don't worry, V. Little Benji is in good hands."

17

LUCKY

"Can I hold him?" Emma asked as soon as we got in the car. "I might not get another chance once Scotty gets his hands on him."

We all laughed. "Sure, here ya go." I passed him up front to Emma. "Thanks for doing this with me, you guys. It means a lot."

"Yeah, it was fun. We should all hang out again some time," Brylee said.

"I'd like that," I said.

"Me, too," Emma agreed and giggled as the puppy licked her chin.

We pulled up to my house, and Brylee said, "Hey, how about tonight? I know this great party. You two want to tag along?"

"Really?" I asked. "Sure."

"Yeah!" Emma said.

"Okay, cool. It'll be mostly seniors, but you should be okay. Just try to dress a little older, and maybe wear makeup."

Emma and I scrunched our noses up.

"Look, I know you don't like wearing makeup," Brylee said, "but make an exception this once. Please. For me."

"I guess so," I said.

"Okay," Emma agreed.

"Good, that's settled," Brylee said. "Let's unload this stuff so we can leave, and so you can go surprise your little brother with his new puppy."

I punched in the code on the garage door. We unloaded Brylee's car, hiding it all in the garage before the big reveal. Brylee said she'd come back in two hours to pick me up, then she and Emma left.

I closed the garage and entered the house through the front door, careful to keep the puppy hidden under a fleece blanket Suzie had given me as part of the pet adoption. Since I didn't see anyone around, I searched for something to put the puppy in. I found a laundry basket sitting on the end of the couch, filled with clean, unfolded laundry. I grabbed the basket, dumped the clothes onto the couch, and put the puppy inside. Then I spread the blanket over the top of the basket and put it on the floor, next to the couch. I kept one hand on the blanket in case the puppy tried to get out. "Hello? Is anybody home? Scotty? Mom? Dad? Where is everyone?"

Scotty bounded down the stairs, jumping over the last three and landing with a thud. "We're all here, V. Why are you shouting? Are you okay?"

"I didn't mean to worry you, Scotty. Of course I'm okay. Everything's fine. I want to show you something, that's all. Where's Mom and Dad?"

"Here we are," Mom said as she and Dad walked in from the kitchen.

"What's all the excitement about?" Dad asked.

"Why are you sitting on the floor, V?" Scotty's eyes flitted from me to the laundry basket. "What's in that basket? And why is it moving?"

"That's what I want to show you. Are you ready?"

"Is it a surprise? Is it for me? What is it? Is it a puppy? Did you get me a puppy? Oh, V, did you get me a puppy? I'm so excited! Show me, show me, show me!"

"Settle down there, little man," Dad said. "Don't get too excited; you don't want to scare what's under the blanket."

"Yes, sweetie. Why don't you sit down on the couch so V can show you her surprise," Mom said.

"Okay, is everyone ready?" I asked, looking at my family.

Mom smiled, and Dad winked.

Scotty took a deep breath and let it out slowly. In a calm, steady voice that surprised me, he said, "Yes, I am ready." His little hands were folded on his lap, his eyes were wide, and he did his best to sit as still as possible.

I picked up the laundry basket and sat down on the couch next to Scotty, with the basket on my lap. I inched the blanket off the basket to reveal the furry bundle inside. The puppy put his paws up on the edge and peered out. I picked him up and placed him on Scotty's lap. Scotty held him and laughed and cried and giggled all at once. "Is this for me?" he asked with tears in his eyes. "Is this my puppy?"

"Yes, Scotty. Meet your new puppy," I said.

"He's so cute! I love him! Where did you get him?"

"He's a rescue puppy. His owner couldn't keep him anymore, so he ended up in an animal shelter. The shelter called the pet rescue where my friend volunteers, and my friend has been fostering him in her home. She knew he'd be the perfect companion for you. I went over to get him before someone else got him."

Scotty jumped up, causing the puppy to fall on the floor. Scotty wrapped his arms around me without noticing. The puppy was a little dazed but otherwise fine. Mom picked up the puppy and told Scotty to sit back down. She explained how he had to be calm and slow and gentle, not to scare the puppy or hurt him. After Scotty apologized, Mom looked at him and asked, "What are you going to name him?"

"I'm gonna call him Lucky!"

"Lucky, huh? Why the name Lucky?"

"Because V rescued him just like you rescued me. His first owner couldn't keep him, and now we get to adopt him, just like my first daddy couldn't keep me after my first mommy died. But you rescued me. You adopted me. I have a second mommy and a second daddy who love me. I got a second chance, and that makes me lucky."

Mom's jaw dropped open, tears welling up in her eyes.

Mine did, too.

"I also have a really cool big sister who brings me great surprises!" Scotty gently took the puppy off his lap this time and placed him on the couch. He stood up and launched himself onto my lap, throwing his arms around me. "I already love Lucky so much, just like I love you!"

"I love you, too, squirt."

"Hey, I told you not to call me that."

"What kind of a big sister would I be if I didn't at least tease you a little now and then, huh?"

"And what kind of a little brother would I be if I never let you play with Lucky when you call me a squirt?" Scotty scowled.

We all laughed, the loud laughter of love and joy that causes tears to slide out of the corners of your eyes. The sudden noise startled the puppy, and he yelped.

We laughed even more.

"Welcome to the family, Lucky!"

18

THE PARTY

18

THE PARTY

Three hours later, Brylee and Emma showed up at my front door. They came in to see Lucky, and make polite conversation with my parents, then we said our goodbyes and headed for the car. Brylee apologized for being late and said it had something to do with Santi. He was having a rough day and needed to see her, so she told him to meet us at the party, after they'd talked on the phone for an hour.

As soon as we got to the party at some guy named Steve's house, Brylee met up with Santi and they disappeared, leaving Emma and me to fend for ourselves in a house full of half-drunk seniors. We were more than a little intimidated. We found a quiet place on the couch in the living room, as most people were surrounding the keg in the kitchen or hanging out in the backyard. We felt like we shouldn't really be there and wanted to leave, but we had no idea where Brylee was. We tried to make the best of it, so we sort of blended into the background, taking it all in.

A cute guy walked up to us and handed us each a beer. "Are you girls old enough to drink?" he asked, winking. He sat down next to us and leaned over conspiratorially. "That's okay. I'm not either." He took a long drink and laughed like that was the funniest thing he'd ever said. "I'm Steve. I live here. I don't remember ever seeing you two around before. What's your deal?"

"We came with Brylee," Emma said, as if that explained everything.

"Oh, Brylee's cool. Okay, have fun, girls." Steve got up to leave, then stopped and turned around. "Wait a minute. I know you." He pointed at me. "You're that teacher's kid. The English teacher with breast cancer."

"Don't say that. Take it back," I shot back. "Her cancer's all gone. Besides, my mom would freak if she knew people referred to her as 'the teacher with cancer.' She's so much more than her stupid cancer diagnosis!"

"Okay, okay, sorry. Geesh. Have a nice night, ladies." He tipped his glass at us and left us there to drink our beers one tiny sip at a time, making them last so we wouldn't get buzzed.

We sat in silence, at least ten feet away from anyone else at the party. I couldn't even look at Emma because it was all I could do not to run out of there. I didn't understand why I'd had such a strong reaction to Steve's comment. He didn't say anything bad about my mom; he just repeated what he'd heard —that she had cancer. Which was true. She *did* have cancer. *But did she still have it? Could it come back?* No, I couldn't bring myself to think these things. I just wanted to go home. Coming here was a stupid idea. No one wanted to talk to us lowly sophomores.

I was about to suggest we should look for Brylee and leave when the hottest guy in our school walked over to us. I put my hand on Emma's knee and squeezed, widening my eyes like, 'oh my gosh, I cannot believe this is happening.' Ken Dern sat down beside me and said, "Hey, V, it's great to see you here. How've you been?"

OMG, Ken Dern knows my name? He knows who I am? I was freaking out inside. Okay, when I say Ken was the hottest guy in the entire high school, it might sound biased, but it's true. At least all the girls I'd heard talking about him thought so. He had shaggy, sandy blond hair, tan skin, a ruggedly handsome face and square jaw, and ice blue eyes. The kind of eyes that pierced my soul.

Guys like Ken Dern never noticed girls like me. They noticed Emma and Brylee, who were both way prettier than me. I was still skinny and underdeveloped, didn't wear makeup, and didn't have a clue how to talk to the opposite sex. Most of the time, I was just plain rude to Crash. *Crash? Why am I thinking about Crash?* I shook my head, focusing on the ridiculously attractive guy in front of me. Did he really remember me?

When Emma and I were in sixth grade and Ken was in eighth grade, he used to ride a minibike in a nearby vacant field with his brother, Keith. They made jumps and ramps out of the hills and dips in the field. Emma and I played there sometimes; it was only a few blocks from her house. There was a big construction sign on a post when we'd entered the field, but it's not there anymore. They built houses on it.

Anyway, one glorious day, Keith pulled up beside us and asked Emma if she wanted a ride. She hopped on the back of his bike, and they took off. A few minutes later, Ken pulled up and asked if *I* wanted a ride! I could hardly contain my excitement. I got to ride on a motorbike with a boy. I wrapped my arms around his waist and held on for dear life. I loved the thrill of the ride, the feel of the wind rushing past my face, and being that close to a boy—all at once.

That was probably the highlight of my little eleven-year-old life; my first crush began that day, just because Ken had been nice to me. Even though he'd treated me like a little kid, he had been very kind. He had paid attention to *me*, and it had felt really good.

Not long after that day, Ken's family had moved across town, and we never saw them in the field again. I didn't see him again until last year when I ran into him in the hallway by my locker. As soon as I realized it was him, I blushed crimson and ran off before he could say anything.

"V?" Emma poked me with her elbow. "Ken asked you a question."

"Huh? Oh, sorry." I felt my face flush.

"You still ride on the back of other people's bikes?" he teased.

Oh my gosh, he does remember me! "I can't believe you remember that," I said. "I was just a little kid back then."

"Well, you're not a little kid now." He gave me an approving once-over and scooted a little closer.

Emma rolled her eyes and said, "I'm going to go get a refill. Anybody want anything?"

I shook my head. She got up and gave me a disapproving glance before turning away and walking toward the kitchen.

Ken put his arm around me. "I have to tell you something," he whispered in my ear.

"What?"

"Not here. It's too loud. Let's go upstairs where it's quieter."

"But—"

"Don't worry," he interrupted. "Steve's cool. He's a good buddy of mine, so he won't mind. Besides, he has a cool pet iguana I want to show you."

Ken took me by the hand and led me upstairs. My skin

came alive at his touch. *I'm holding hands with a boy!* I felt just like I had on that day, on the back of his minibike . . . all over again. Yes, at fifteen, when it came to boys, I was still very much a child.

When we got upstairs and entered Steve's room, Ken didn't bother to show me the iguana. He sat on Steve's bed and patted the spot next to him. I walked over and sat on the bed, too, inches away. He reached over with both hands and turned my shoulders to face him. "How long has it been, V?"

"Since the minibike ride? Uh, four years."

"Four years, huh? We were so young. And look at you now; you're so beautiful."

"Y-y-you think I'm beautiful?" *Get a grip! I can't believe I'm stuttering.*

"Yes, V, I do. Your eyes are like cat eyes, dazzling and seductive all at once. Stunning."

Before I had time to react to that, he pulled me in and kissed me. It was soft and warm, tender. Then he parted his lips, so I parted mine. He stuck his tongue in my mouth, and I pulled away. "Stop it! What are you doing?"

"What's the big deal? We're just kissing. What's wrong? Haven't you ever been kissed before?"

"No."

"Oh, well, in that case . . . let me show you how. It'll be easier if you lay down."

"On the bed?"

"Of course, where else?" He laughed. "Don't be nervous. It's okay. I've been told I'm a very good teacher."

I took my shoes off and repositioned myself on the bed, lying on my back with my head on the pillow. Ken kicked his shoes off, too, and slowly lowered himself on top of me. It felt surreal. *Is this really happening?* His lips brushed mine as he told me to relax, to just follow his lead. He parted my lips with his tongue, explored my mouth with it, and I tentatively darted my tongue into his mouth, tasting his tongue, then retreating. It felt strange, foreign, yet thrilling, too. But this was a different kind of thrilling than that minibike ride. Very different.

Once I got the kissing down, he took off his T-shirt and then took my hand and put it on the hard bulge of his jeans.

I gasped.

"Do you want to touch it?"

"Uh . . ."

"I can show you how. It's okay . . ." He pushed himself up off of me and kneeled on the bed, unbuttoning his jeans.

My eyes grew wide, and my stomach suddenly ached. I felt sweaty and nauseous, panicky. I wasn't excited anymore. I wasn't ready for this. I didn't know how to get out of it. I didn't know what to say. My voice seemed stuck in my throat. I wanted to run, but I was frozen in place. I couldn't move, and I didn't know what to do.

Ken reached for my hand again, and I recoiled.

He laughed. "It won't bite, you know." He pushed his jeans down to his knees, tucked his thumbs into his navy briefs and circled the waistband, inching them down slowly. I'd never seen bikini underwear on a guy before. It looked so weird. After all, my dad wore boxers.

The door exploded open, and Emma charged in. I had never been so happy to see her in my life. Was that fear in her eyes?

"There you are, V. I've been looking all over for you. Brylee is super sick, and we have to get her home. Come on, let's go. Now."

Her voice had an edge to it. Was she mad at me? I didn't understand.

"V, get up, put your shoes on, and let's go," she seethed.

I looked at Ken. "Sorry," I whispered. I got off the bed, sat down on the floor, and slipped my sandals on. I looked back up at Ken. He was already fully dressed and looking pissed. I followed Emma downstairs. Brylee was outside, puking in the flower garden.

"She can't drive. V, you have to drive," Emma said.

"Me? I can't drive!"

"You've been taking driving lessons."

"But just as an observer. He doesn't let me drive, not till my half birthday."

"Your half birthday?"

"Fifteen-and-a-half, when I can get a driver's permit."

"Oh."

More retching from Brylee.

"Well, *she* clearly can't drive. Look, you hear what the instructor tells the other students, right?"

"Yeah . . ."

"Then you know more than me. Now help me get her in the back seat." Determined, Emma kneeled down to help Brylee. "Where are your keys?"

"In the visor," Brylee said.

"What?"

"I got it," I said. "The car's unlocked. She hid them so she wouldn't have to carry them. Come on, let's get her in the car."

Emma and I braced ourselves on either side of Brylee and pulled her up to her feet. We half dragged her to her car, which wasn't easy considering that she was five-foot-nine to our smaller five-foot-two frames. We put her in the back seat. She was mostly incoherent and mumbling, but I heard Santi's name a couple times. I wondered where he was.

I opened the driver's door, got in, pulled down the sun visor, and the keys fell into my lap. With shaking hands, I picked up the keys and realized the car key was a fob (keyless ignition). I put the keys in the center consul and looked for the start engine button. I didn't see one anywhere.

"Where's the ignition switch?"

"There isn't one."

"What? How the heck do you start the car?"

"Put your foot on the brake," Brylee slurred.

"Which one's the brake?"

"Seriously?" Emma shrieked. "Haven't you learned anything?"

I shot her a look. "I've never been behind the wheel before. This is a lot different than reading a stupid manual." I stomped down on the right pedal. Nothing happened. I depressed the pedal on the left. The engine came to life, and the headlights turned on.

"Whoa." I took a deep breath. "Um, how do I put it in reverse?"

"Unbelievable! I mean—" Emma started.

I cut her off. "Do you want to drive?"

She turned away from me and looked out the window.

"Didn't think so. Now, if you can't tell me where reverse is, then shut up."

Somehow, after what felt like an eternity, and a lot of lurching, I managed to get Brylee home alive.

19

RED AND BLUE LIGHTS

When I dropped Brylee off, she was coherent enough to thank me and said I could drive myself home, and that she'd pick up her car tomorrow when she'd sobered up. Driving Emma home was another matter. I wasn't comfortable driving Brylee's car at all; I didn't want to drive any more than I had to.

As if Emma could read my thoughts, she said, "You know, my mom thinks I'm spending the night at Brylee's. She'd be full of questions if I came home now. Maybe I could crash at your place tonight?"

"Oh, thank goodness. Yes, that would be great. Let me concentrate on getting us home in one piece, and then we can talk."

"Sounds good."

We rode in silence for maybe a minute, if that, when I saw flashing red and blue lights behind me. "Oh no! Emma, I think I'm being pulled over. What should I do?"

"Pull over!"

"But I'll get in trouble for driving without a license."

"You'll be in trouble for a lot more than that if you don't pull over."

The siren whirred, and I jumped. I eased the car over to the curb and put it in park. The police officer walked up to the driver's side and peered in the window with a flashlight as I fumbled with the buttons on the door to roll down the window.

"Good evening, officer," I managed, trying to sound mature.

"License and registration, please," he said, all business.

I gulped. I didn't even have a learner's permit or a state ID card. All I had was my school ID. This was bad. "Oh, darn, I'm so sorry. I left it at home. You see, we were—"

"Registration then," he said, cutting me off.

Emma opened the glovebox and got out the registration. Fortunately, it was sitting on top of other papers and a few napkins, easy to find. She handed it over to me, and I gave it to the officer.

He took the registration from me and said, "Wait here. Stay inside the car. I'll be right back."

"What is he doing?" Emma asked.

"He's probably running the tags to see if there's any outstanding warrants on the car," I guessed.

We waited.

The officer came back and said, "Ma'am, I'm going to have to ask you to step outside the car."

Ma'am? At least he didn't think I was too young to drive. I glanced at Emma, and she shrugged. Not helpful. I stepped out of the car. He told me to walk a straight line, heel to toe. *Oh no! He thinks I'm drunk! I only had half a beer. Less than that, even. Will it show up if he makes me take a breathalyzer? Think, think! Am I about to be arrested for drunk driving? Crap. My mom is going to kill me!*

"Do you know why I pulled you over tonight, Miss Rossi?"

Miss R—oh, he thinks I'm Brylee. It's her name on the registra-tion. Duh. "No, sir. I wasn't speeding. I was on a residential street, going slow."

"Yes, you were going slow. Very slow. Did you know that driving under the posted speed limit can be just as dangerous as speeding? It's also a sign of intoxication. Have you been drinking tonight, Miss Rossi?"

"No, I . . ."

His phone buzzed. He checked it and immediately drew his gun. "Hold it right there! Turn around and place your hands on the hood of the car."

"Why? What's going on?"

"I'm asking the questions here. Turn around! Who are you? What have you done with Brylee Rossi? Why are you driving her car? Who's that in the passenger seat?"

"I can explain. Please, just let me explain." I placed my trembling hands on the car, tears threatening to spill over. *How does he know?* I cleared my throat. "You're right. I'm not Brylee. This is her car. I had to drive her home because she was too dr —uh, sick, to drive. She said I could drive her car home. My friend and I are sober. We were trying to do the right thing by not letting Brylee drive. We're just trying to get home safely."

He walked to the car and faced me, shining the flashlight in my eyes. "Why were you driving so slow if you're sober?"

When all else fails, go for honesty. Here we go . . . "Because I'm only fifteen," I said, squinting at the bright light. "I've had two driving lessons; neither were behind the wheel of an actual car. They were part of a group lesson, and I had to sit in the back seat. This is my first time driving. Can you please shine that light away from my eyes? You're scaring me."

"Sorry." He pointed his flashlight away. "Wait a sec. You're just a kid? Great. Now what am I going to do, slap you with reckless endangerment, driving without a license, and being a minor driving a minor? You won't be able to get your license, or even your permit, for a full year. Maybe not even till you're eighteen."

"Can they really do that?" This was not going well. Then I caught the name on his badge. *A. Lomeli.* In spite of the mess I was in, I grinned. My fear dissolving, I now knew what to do. My heart stopped racing. In a strong, clear voice, I said, "It's okay, Alan. No one has to know."

"What? How do you know my name? What's going on here?"

"I know that you're Officer Alan Lomeli, age twenty-two, and a rookie cop. I know that you're fresh out of the academy and you shouldn't even be on patrol without a veteran officer. You're out alone—by yourself—unsupervised. I think my very good friend, Detective Andrew Lomeli, would love to hear about this."

"No, you can't be serious. Please don't tell Uncle Andrew."

I smiled and winked. "I won't if you won't."

"I knew it! I had a feeling it was you. My uncle told me about you, too, Miss Jiménez. He told me to keep an eye out for the smart-aleck redheaded kid with a penchant for sticking her nose where it doesn't belong. So when I pulled you over and you didn't have a license on you, and as far as I knew, you were claiming to be Brylee Rossi, I had her driver's license photo sent over."

"Ah, and that's when you pulled a gun on me and scared me half to death."

"Hey, a rookie can't be too careful. Clearly, you are not five-foot-nine with black hair and dark brown eyes."

"Clearly."

We eyed each other, neither one of us backing down.

"Can we go now, officer?" Emma called out from the car. "I really have to pee."

"All right, get your friend home safe. I'll let you off with a warning this time. But I don't want to see you driving again until you're legal, understand?"

"Yes, sir, and I don't want to see you patrolling by yourself again until you're legal."

"Hey, watch it. Boy, my uncle was right about you. You better watch that mouth of yours, young lady. I suggest you go before I change my mind and write you up for a whole list of infractions."

"Good night, Officer Lomeli. Thank you for the warning." I smiled and waved, then got in the car and pushed the gas too fast, causing the car to lurch forward, before speeding off.

When we finally got home—without a scratch, I might add —Emma gave me a big hug as soon as we got out of the car. She thanked me for the tenth time for driving us, and for talking my way out of a ticket. We went inside and tiptoed up the stairs. It was late, and everyone was in bed. By the time we went to my room, I didn't know whether to laugh or to cry. I was relieved and exhausted. It had been a strange night, but I was so happy Emma was here. I was beyond happy to have my best friend back.

"I'm still mad at you, by the way," Emma said as she flung herself on my bed.

Great, what did I do now? I just got her back. "You are?"

"Yep. What were you thinking, going upstairs with Ken like that?"

I exhaled deeply, not realizing I'd been holding my breath. "Oh, that."

"Don't give me 'oh, that' like it's no big deal. I just saved your life tonight, and I didn't even get a thank you."

"What are you talking about? I was fine. We were just kissing."

"Yeah, right, and I didn't just see the guy with his shirt off, jeans down to his knees, and about to pull his thing out of his tight little undies."

"I was about to tell him to stop when you walked in. I had it under control."

"Geez, V, you really don't know, do you?"

"Know what?"

"Don't be so naive. He wasn't going to stop. He *never* stops. He had you up there for one thing, and one thing only. Ken Dern pressures girls to have sex with him."

"That's not true! He was nice to me."

"How do you think these guys catch their prey? They're always nice—at first. I bet he told you how pretty you were, too."

My face flushed.

"You don't get it, V. He preys on innocent girls. That's his thing. He doesn't take no for an answer. He tells them whatever he thinks they want to hear to get the gold. Then he goes back to school and brags to his buddies about his latest conquest. Why do you think everyone calls Shawna Stone a slut? Ken ruined her, and her reputation."

"I thought he liked me," I whispered. "We had a connection. Remember that day at the field? When we rode the minibikes with Ken and his brother? I really thought I was different . . . special."

"I'm so sorry, V. I shouldn't have told you like this, but you needed to know. Come here." Emma opened her arms and wiggled her fingers.

I sat on the bed next to her, letting her cradle me in her arms. I felt worthless, ashamed, and used.

"I bet he used that minibike memory to get to you, too, didn't he?"

I nodded and sniffed.

"What an asshole."

"Why would he do that to me?"

"Not just to you—he wants to have sex with as many girls as he can. He doesn't care about any of them. He has no respect for women. He's sick. Makes me wonder what his parents are like, ya know?"

"Yeah. He was probably dropped on his head a few times when he was little and now he's just not right in the head."

We both laughed. It felt so good to laugh.

I told Emma everything that night. We talked all night and caught each other up on all the things we'd missed out on over the last year. I told her about last night's break-in, Pedro's threats, the gangs, Brylee's boyfriend Santi . . . all of it. It felt so good to be able to talk to her again, the way we used to before. Before, you know, the kidnappings. She helped me devise a plan to lie low and try to stay under the radar.

I hoped that Pedro wouldn't see me as a threat, that he'd just forget about me and my family. Truthfully, I hoped he'd leave town and go somewhere far, far away—or better yet, that he'd finally be arrested and taken off the streets so he couldn't hurt anyone anymore. Whatever happened with Pedro and his gang, at least I finally had someone to talk to about it all, someone who'd have my back no matter what. My best friend. Emma.

20

EMMA'S BACK

I lay in a pasture, gazing up at the cloudless blue sky. The sound of a child's laughter wafted on the breeze toward me. I smiled. I closed my eyes and felt the warmth of the sun's rays kiss my face. Then a dark shadow passed over me, and an enormous cow licked my nose! "What the—?"

I woke up. Scotty stood over me, giggling his head off while Lucky danced on my chest, licking my nose.

"Good morning, V! Good morning, Emma! Lucky says it's time for you two to get up! You have to see the new trick he can do!" Scotty exclaimed.

"Good morning to you, too, squirt!" Emma jumped out of bed and ran over to Scotty, tickling him.

More giggling ensued. "Emma! Stop it," Scotty said, breathless. "Don't call me squirt."

I rubbed my eyes and yawned. "When did we fall asleep?"

"Around six, I think," Emma said.

"Mm, what time is it now?" I squinted at the clock on my nightstand.

"It's nine already, sleepyheads. Come on, Mom made breakfast."

"Well, I guess we got about three hours of sleep. Are you hungry?"

"Famished."

I tried to glare at my little brother, but he was too cute, giggling and waving his hands around as he deflected Lucky's kisses and puppy nips on his chin. I shook my head and accepted that I wasn't going to get any more sleep for a while. "Okay, Scotty, we'll be right down. You can show us Lucky's trick after breakfast."

"Yay! You better hurry up. Mom made your favorite pancakes, and I might eat them all!"

"You better not!" I roared.

Scotty squealed and took off for the stairs, with Lucky trailing after him.

Emma wore my sweats down to breakfast. We always used to borrow each other's clothes, so I didn't think anything of it. I grabbed the peanut butter out of the pantry and sat down at the kitchen table, focusing on the heaping plate of pancakes in front of me. Scotty was already at the table, shoveling forkfuls of pancake into his mouth at lightning speed.

"Good morning, girls," Mom said, adding bacon and maple syrup to the table. "It's so good to see you, Emma. It's been a while."

"Hi Hannah. It's good to see you, too," Emma said.

We'd always called each other's moms by their first names for as long as I could remember. Rosa had insisted on it, and my mom didn't care. Her students called her Mrs. J at school, so I think she liked it when my friends called her Hannah instead.

"Where's Dad?" I asked as Mom sat down to eat with us.

"He had a meeting with the other soccer coaches in Scotty's

league. He should be home in a couple hours." She finished chewing a bite of bacon, then said, "Emma, how is your mom? I've been meaning to call Rosa for a while now. Please tell her I've been thinking of her. With the new school year starting up again, I guess I sort of lost track of time."

"It's okay. She understands," Emma said. "She knows how busy teachers are at the beginning of the year. Actually, my mom is doing really well. She just got promoted to a shift supervisor at Costco."

"That's wonderful," Mom said. "And your abuela?"

"Abuela's good. She likes to play bingo on Thursday nights with her friends. They're all her age, but she calls them 'the girls.' They're really cute together."

"Is everyone done eating breakfast yet?" Scotty asked. "You guys are taking forever, and I want to show you the new trick I taught Lucky!"

"I'm done, Scotty," Emma said. "You can show me."

"Yay! Come on, V. Hurry."

"Okay, okay, I'm coming." We got up from the table and followed Scotty outside to the backyard.

"Go on, kids, don't worry about helping me clean up," Mom said, winking.

"Watch this," Scotty said. "Here, Lucky! Here boy," he called and patted his legs. Lucky ran over to Scotty, jumped up on him and nearly knocked him over.

"Good job!" I said. "You taught him to come when you call him. That's great."

"But wait, that's not all," Scotty said, pushing Lucky down. "He can also fetch. Watch this." Scotty threw a rubber ball across the yard and said, "Go get it, Lucky!"

Lucky ran toward the ball, past it, and kept going all the way to the back fence. Scotty's shoulders slumped.

"That's okay, Scotty. Give him a little more time. He'll get it," Emma said, tousling his hair.

"Yeah, I guess," Scotty said. "But guess what else?"

"What else?" I asked.

"I got all the P's down!"

"What do you mean?"

"You know, the P's: potty, poop, and play. That's practically all Lucky does."

"What about eat and sleep?" Emma asked. "Don't puppies sleep a lot?"

"Yeah, but I couldn't think of a P word for those."

"Hmm, how about pig out and pass out?" Emma suggested.

"Oh yeah, those are good ones!" I said. "It's the five P's of puppy training: potty, poop, play, pig out, and pass out! Over and over again, all day."

"You're silly, V," Scotty said, giggling.

"I know I am but you're a squirt," I shot back.

"V, stop calling me that!" Scotty yelled, frowning.

"It's okay, Scotty. I know how to get her back," Emma said, her eyes dancing with mischief.

"How?"

"A tickle attack!"

Emma and Scotty chased me around the backyard with Lucky nipping at our heels, all of us laughing. *It feels so good to have my Emma back!*

PART TWO

21
NEW ATTITUDE

THREE MONTHS LATER

IT WAS MID-DECEMBER, finals week. Visions of Christmas and winter break were dancing in my head. I had my Emma back, and our bond was stronger than ever. We had plenty to be merry about!

Just as I'd hoped, Pedro and his gang left me alone. There were still a few break-ins here and there, but I kept my nose out of it. I was done with the teen detective biz. I mean, who did I think I was, anyway? Veronica Mars? She wasn't *real*, just a made-up character on a TV show. I had to face the truth. And the truth was, I cared more about my family and my friends—and my own life—than a little gang activity, or crime spree, in the neighborhood. Besides, Detective Lomeli told me plenty of times before to "just be a kid and leave the crime-solving stuff to the police." So, I was only doing what I was told.

After a few days of Crash begging me to stay in Mr. C's driving class, my refusal, and then blatantly ignoring him, he finally got the message and left me alone, too. Life was good. Emma and I were about to get our driver's permits!

Since our half birthday was on Christmas Eve (Emma was my birthday twin, June 24th), we would have to wait until the Tuesday after Christmas to get our permits, when the DMV opened again. But no worries. I was just excited I'd finally get to drive, legally. Emma and I were already signed up for new driving classes, starting up again January 3rd, also our first day back at school after break.

I'd hoped for a different instructor or driving school, but Mr. C cut me a deal. He let Emma and me take the six-hour behind-the-wheel course together. He seemed to prefer more than one student at a time, anyway. We just had to keep track of our driving instruction hours until we each reached the required six hours.

But I'm getting ahead of myself. As I mentioned, it was the middle of finals week, and I had a grueling final in AP Euro after lunch. I had planned on studying in the library all through lunch, but my plans don't always work out.

When the bell rang, I headed for the library, determined not to let anyone or anything get in my way.

"V, stop!" Emma blazed a trail through the people in the hall to get to me, nearly mowing them down. By the look on her face, she was in no mood to hear me say, 'I can't talk to you right now. I have a final to study for.' I braced myself for whatever had her so wound up.

"I'm worried about Brylee," she said, catching up to me.

I sighed. Ever since Emma and I started hanging out again, Brylee stopped hanging out with Emma. At first I thought it was because she didn't like me, but Emma assured me Brylee just wanted to spend all her free time with her boyfriend, Santi. I knew I should warn her about him, but he'd told me he wanted out of the gang. He practically begged me not to tell Brylee and said she was the best thing that had ever happened to him. Since I told Emma nearly everything, we went back and forth over telling Brylee about Santi. She reluctantly had agreed not to, for now. But . . . Santi wouldn't let Brylee get hurt, would he? *I'm putting a lot of faith in him.*

I was selfishly glad to go back to the way things had been before Brylee and Emma had ever crossed paths. I felt like a horrible human being admitting to myself that their kidnapping and unlikely friendship had inconvenienced me, but there it was. I was glad Brylee finally had her own friends; Emma was mine. "Emma, can this wait? I—"

"No, it cannot. I have to talk to you right now. I think it's a matter of life and death."

That got my attention. A pit of guilt formed in my stomach. *If Santi has put her in danger, I'll never forgive myself.* "What do you mean, 'life and death'?" I searched her eyes, silently hoping that she was exaggerating, that this was not serious. "Talk to me. What's this about?"

"Not here. We have to go somewhere quiet. I have to show you something."

"We can go to the library."

"No, not the library. Let's go outside. I think better when I'm outside."

"Okay, you got it." I followed Emma till we got outside, heading toward the track. As we walked, Emma took out her phone and pulled something up on the screen.

"In study hall this morning, I asked Brylee if I could borrow a piece of paper. She handed me her notebook, and I had to flip through a few pages before I found a blank one. But this poem caught my eye. I snapped a quick pic of it, flipped to a blank page, and handed the notebook back to Brylee so she wouldn't be suspicious. It's been bugging me ever since, and it was excruciating to have to wait until lunchtime to show you. This is clearly a cry for help, don't you think so? Do you think she's suicidal?"

"Wait a sec. Let me read it first, okay?"

"Oh, sorry." Emma handed me her phone. I read the neat handwriting on the photographed notebook paper.

I need to be needed

I need to be loved

I want to be with someone who wants to be with me

not someone who shuts me out.

I want a normal, healthy, loving relationship,

and all that goes with it.

I want your love

I need your attention

I crave your affection.

No more lies

No more excuses

No more ghosting me!

What's the point of being together if we're never together?

What's the point of living?

"Wow, that last line is chilling," I said, handing back Emma's phone. I couldn't believe what I'd just read. Was Brylee actually suicidal? I didn't know what to do. I didn't know she and Santi were having problems. "Do you know where she is now?"

"She said she had a doctor appointment to go to, but honestly, I think she ditched after study hall. I have no idea where she is, and she's not answering her phone. I'm really worried about her, V."

"Yeah, me, too."

"Plus, about a week ago, I saw bumps and scabs on her lower back. When I asked her about them, she just brushed me off and said they were from mosquito bites. She said they were itchy and she had kept scratching them, which is why they looked so bad. But how would she get mosquito bites on her back? Doesn't that seem strange to you? It was really weird, and she acted odd when I pointed it out. I feel like she's hiding something from us."

"I think she's been acting strange, too, but then again, I've always thought she was a bit strange. I mean, no offense, but she's always been standoffish and cold, at least to me."

"She's not. If you took the time to actually get to know her, you'd see that," Emma huffed.

"Sorry. You're right."

Emma glared at me.

"Really, I'm sorry, okay?"

Emma nodded.

"So where would she go if she's not with Santi and she's not at a doctor appointment? Would she go home?"

"No, definitely not. She's supposed to be at school, remember? Her mom is there. Besides, she's hardly ever there if she can help it. Her little sisters bug her too much, and her brother is a jerk; she never gets any peace."

"Her brother's name is Cory, right? Isn't he our age? Why doesn't he go to our school?"

"Their mom put him in a strict, private boarding school because his grades were slipping. He hates it there and releases his bad attitude all over his sisters every chance he gets. Brylee says he's a pain in the ass to deal with when he's home. No, she definitely wouldn't go home."

"Ugh. Speaking of grades . . . sorry, Em, but I gotta go. I have a huge final next period, and I need to go over my notes at least once. Keep thinking about where she might be, and we'll look for her after school, okay?"

"With what wheels? Our bikes?"

"Sure, if that's what it takes."

Emma laughed. "Brylee used to be my ride. Man, I can't wait till I get my license."

"Me, too. Me, too. Well, wish me luck?"

"Good luck on your test."

DURING THE FINAL, I felt my phone buzz. I'd forgotten to take it out of my back pocket. Thankfully, it was on vibrate. Mr. Feta didn't hear it. But I was dying to read the text. *Did Emma hear from Brylee? Was she okay?* I couldn't concentrate and had to take a couple deep, calming breaths to try to focus on the test.

Luckily, I'd studied enough and didn't need that cram session in the library after all. I answered the test questions easily and with confidence, which was good because AP Euro was not my best subject. I silently sent up a little 'thank you' prayer that Mr. Feta had made the final easy; it was practically word-for-word straight from the study guide.

After I turned in my test, I got a book out of my backpack and then snuck my phone out and put it in the book. I opened the book carefully and peered at my phone's screen. It was a text from Brylee.

> I know about Santi. And I know you know.
> Meet me in the senior lot after school and
> don't bring Emma

K

My stomach did a couple flips as I tucked my phone back in my pocket. I would have to be careful. I didn't know how mad she was. Plus, if she really was suicidal, she wasn't in her right mind. I didn't want to be the one to push her over the edge.

22

BRYLEE

I hesitated as I walked to the senior parking lot because I had no idea where Brylee parked. She saw me before I saw her and sped toward me. I jumped out of the way before she screeched to a stop next to me. Did I really want to get in the car with a possibly suicidal maniac?

"Get in," Brylee commanded. The passenger door flew open as if by magic.

But then I noticed Brylee straightening up and realized she had pushed it open. Against my better judgment, I got in the car.

Without waiting for me to put my seat belt on, she sped off. She didn't even stop at the stop sign at the end of the school property. She just threw on her signal and turned right without looking. *This is not how I thought I'd die.*

"Brylee, slow down!" I shouted. "You're making me nervous."

She gripped the steering wheel tighter and kept her eyes on the road, but she did slow down a bit. "Sorry. A lot is going on, and I need answers. I'm hoping you have them."

"Okay?"

"Not yet. Wait till I park first . . . for the safety of *both* of us."

"Thank you. I really don't want to die today."

"Ha ha, very funny," she said as she turned the radio up, most likely to tune out my complaints.

When Brylee pulled into a strip mall parking lot a few minutes later, she parked the car at the end of a deserted row. We were surrounded by empty parking spaces. She rolled down all the windows and killed the ignition, which turned off the blaring music.

I watched in silence as she took off her seat belt, turned her body toward me, and folded her hands in her lap.

I took her cue and did the same, mimicking her.

After an uncomfortable pause, she said, "Spill it."

"Spill what? I don't understand."

"Tell me what you know about Santi's involvement with the Pico 7 gang."

Oh. That. "What do you know?"

"Don't play games with me, V. Santi told me he told you everything. He didn't have time to tell me, so he said you'd fill me in. Imagine my surprise when I found out my *friend* has been keeping this secret from me."

I gulped. "He didn't have time? What do you mean?"

"I'm asking the questions right now, not you."

"Right. Sorry. Where should I start? I mean, I don't know how much you already know."

"Why did Santi tell you about the gang and not me? Why couldn't he trust me?"

"He loves you. He was afraid that if you knew, you'd break up with him. He was terrified of losing you. He wanted to get out of the gang and was hoping he could walk away before you found out. He wanted to be a good person. He said you made him want to be a good person."

"Who's Pedro?"

I looked at her, confused. "You don't know who Pedro is?"

"I need you to tell me."

"Pedro is the leader of the Pico 7 gang . . . and he's Santi's older brother."

All the color drained from Brylee's face as she stared at me, her hands balling into fists in her lap.

"Brylee? Are you okay? What's going on? Why couldn't Santi tell you himself?"

"Because Pedro found out about me and forbid Santi to ever see me again."

"Oh, um . . . I'm so sorry. I know he wouldn't want you to find out like this, but I think it's for the best that—"

Brylee had a faraway look in her eyes. She started talking over me, as if she couldn't hear me. As if she were in another world. "Santi was always very secretive around me, so guarded. Plus, he'd disappear for days at a time and then reappear, or he wouldn't call or text me back. And he had really lame excuses, like his aunt was sick, he had car trouble, he lost his phone, his phone died, et cetera. I was a fool and believed every lie. But, like the fool I am, I never took the hint. I kept calling and texting. But last night, Santi left his phone in Pedro's car. Pedro picked it up and saw my text messages. And that was all it took. Santi's secret that he'd been keeping from Pedro—his brother—wow, okay, it's starting to make sense now. Anyway, Santi's secret girlfriend was no longer a secret, thanks to my constant texting. If I had just left him alone like he'd asked me to, none of this would have happened. We'd still be together." She paused, her eyes glistening. Then in barely a whisper, she added, "This is all my fault."

"You didn't know Santi was in a gang. Brylee, none of this is your fault."

"The facts disagree with you, V. As I said, Pedro found out about me because I kept blowing up Santi's phone. He'd kept our relationship a secret for five months. And when he finally asks me for a little space? I freak out and blow up his phone! How could I be so stupid?"

"Again, you didn't do anything wrong."

"Save it. I don't need a pep talk from you. Instead of being happy for Santi, that he'd found a nice girl, Pedro ordered him to break up with me and told him he could never see me again."

"But if he wasn't allowed to see or contact you, how do you know all this?"

"I saw him. After study hall this morning, I saw Santi in the hallway, walking toward the exit. I hid behind a locker and decided to follow him. He grabbed me in the parking lot and put his hand over my mouth. He had crazy eyes. I'd never seen him like that before. He pulled me behind a parked car and forced me to kneel down with him. That's when he told me he was in a gang, that Pedro ordered him to stop seeing me, and to ask you about it. He said he loved me but he had to go, that it was best I lose his number and never contact him again. That it was for my safety."

I nodded and said, "Santi's right. Pedro is dangerous. It's best you stay away from him for a while."

"How long have you known Santi was in a gang? And why didn't you tell me?"

"Santi swore me to secrecy." I fidgeted in my seat, palms getting sweaty.

"Since when are you loyal to anybody, let alone *my* boyfriend?"

"That's not fair," I protested. "It's complicated."

"Uncomplicate it for me." There was a raw animal quality to her voice, sort of a menacing growl. Brylee could be quite intimidating, especially when she was angry. But I had to stand my ground. It was the only way to earn her respect, to let her know she couldn't bully me.

"I was in the middle of a case, finding *your* mom's stolen necklace, remember? I caught Santi robbing a house in my neighborhood, and he promised to help me catch his brother and put him behind bars, in exchange asking that I not tell you about his gang involvement."

"And?"

"And what?"

"Why isn't Pedro behind bars?"

"I dropped the case. After I found your mom's necklace, it didn't matter anymore."

"I don't believe you."

I looked down and picked at my thumbnail then let out a sigh. "Pedro broke into my house and threatened to kill my family. I don't have what it takes to solve this on my own." I admitted. "I'm not even a real detective."

"That didn't stop you from finding Emma and me." She was relentless. "What happened to *that* V? That V was gutsy and unstoppable."

"That V's family wasn't threatened." I looked up at her, my eyes pleading for her to stop. But no such luck.

"I see," she seethed. "So now Pedro gets to keep committing crimes, and you're not going to do anything about it?"

"What do you want from me?" I cried out. "I'm just a kid; at least that's what Lomeli keeps telling me. Let the cops handle it."

"Whatever." She turned around and gazed out the windshield. It seemed we were at an impasse.

"Brylee?" I dared. "Did Santi treat you right?"

"What kind of question is that? Of course he treated me right. Like he told you, he's a good person." She slammed her hand on the dashboard. "He's a good person caught in an impossible situation. I can't believe his stupid brother is forcing him to stay in a gang. This is all so unfair."

"Emma told me she saw bruises on your back?"

Brylee narrowed her eyes at me, slumping her shoulders. "Emma's got a big mouth. And they weren't bruises; they were mosquito bites. Santi didn't lay a hand on me."

"Why would you have mosquito bites on your back?"

"Why don't you mind your own damn business?"

I stared her down.

"Fine. If you must know, Santi and I were fooling around in the woods. I bent over and gave him a BJ; when I did, my shirt rose up in the back. For some reason, mosquitos attacked the exposed skin on my lower back. It's stupid and embarrassing. Satisfied?"

I stifled a giggle, unable to help myself and clapped my hand to my mouth. My cheeks were hot, and I knew my face must be reddening. But since I was being bold, and Brylee was confessing, I decided to push my luck and ask one more question, a question that had been bugging me for over a year. "Why did you get in the van with the guy who kidnapped you? The witness said you went with him . . . willingly."

"Wow, V, you're on a roll, aren't you?" Brylee took a deep breath. We sat in silence for a while before she continued. "I was at the mall when I got a text from an unknown number. The anonymous texter said I was a slut and he could prove it. He said he had a video of me having sex at a party, and he was going to release the video to YouTube if I didn't meet him in the parking lot right then. I bought the sweater I was holding and ran out of there. When I got to the parking lot, the guy told me to get in the van. He said he'd show me the video in the van. I wasn't thinking. I didn't hesitate to get in that van. But as soon as I did, he stabbed me with a needle and knocked me out. Next thing I knew, I was tied up in the back and we were a long way from that parking lot."

"I'm so sorry," I said, averting my eyes. "I don't know what to say."

"You believe him, don't you?"

"What do you mean?"

"You believe there's a sex video out there ... of me."

"You just said there was."

"No, I said that guy said there was. You see, there had been rumors going around about me at school, and I didn't know why. If there was a video out there, I wanted to see it. I wanted to see if it had been photoshopped or something, because it wasn't me. I'd never been to a high school party before then. I didn't even have a social life, much less a boyfriend." She whispered the last part, "I was a virgin then."

Something like horror crossed my face when I realized what she was telling me. *If Brylee was a virgin the day she got in that van . . . that means her kidnappers took her virginity.* It was unthinkable. I realized I had already known on some level, but now I knew for sure.

"I know what you're thinking. You want to know why Emma never talks to you about what happened to us? Because she doesn't want to see the look you're giving me right now. That look would destroy her. It's pity, disgust, and fear, all rolled into one. Those men were heinous, and they did heinous things.

But I don't need people to look at me like that, like I'm damaged goods. So stop it."

My cheeks flushed again, and I looked out my window. I was ashamed of myself. Brylee finally told me something real and vulnerable, and I reacted atrociously. I made her feel like a horrible person. It wasn't her fault. She was not to blame. She was a victim! How could I do that to her? I couldn't let her feel like dirt.

I imagined how I would feel if someone looked at me the way I'd just looked at Brylee. I bowed my head and grimaced. Finally, I squared my shoulders, turned in my seat toward Brylee again, and said, "You're right, Brylee. You didn't deserve the way I looked at you just now. But you're wrong about what was behind the look. I don't judge or blame you. I judged what those monsters did to you. You were an innocent victim and they took away your innocence. I can't begin to imagine how horrific that was. My heart hurts for you and I am deeply sorry if I made you feel bad. You are not damaged goods, Brylee. You are a beautiful, strong, tenacious person, and you will get through this. I'm also sorry I haven't been more empathetic and that I wasn't really there for you and Emma. I want you to know that I'm here now and I'll do my best to be supportive. Can you forgive me?"

Brylee nodded through her tears.

I reached out to her and she allowed me to hug her. I held her in my arms while we openly sobbed together. For the first time, I understood a little better what it felt like to be Brylee Rossi.

23

BRIGHT STARS

Friday had finally arrived—the last day of school before Christmas break. No more finals and no more school for two blissful weeks! Emma and I celebrated by getting boba tea. We savored our drinks while we walked to her house. When we got there, we went straight to Emma's room. We finished our boba tea, lounging on her bed and chatting.

It had been about a year since I'd been to Emma's house. Since we started hanging out again, we usually hung out at my house. I didn't question why. Her room looked exactly the same, right down to the giant posters of Mia Hamm and Taylor Swift adorning the walls. The posters reminded me of the two main differences between Emma and me—athleticism and musical talent. She wanted to be a soccer pro, and she had a great singing voice. I didn't have any skills or talents. Sometimes I wondered what she saw in me.

Emma's mom stood in the doorway. "V! It's so good to see you. Come here and give me a hug." She opened her arms, reaching for me like I was a long-lost relative.

I stood up and hugged her as she crushed me in her embrace. "It's good to see you, too, Rosa."

"You should come over more often. Are you staying for dinner?"

It had been just Emma, her mom, and her grandma for as long as I could remember. Her grandma didn't speak English very well, but her mom did. Their family had moved here from Mexico when Rosa was sixteen. That's also when she met Emma's dad. He died in Afghanistan when Emma was just a baby. Rosa had worked at Costco while Emma's abuela had stayed home to take care of her. She used to joke that it sometimes felt like she had two moms.

"V?" Rosa and Emma stared at me expectantly.

"Huh? Oh, sorry. Um, I'll have to check with my mom first, but I think it should be okay. I'll call her. She hates when I text." I took out my phone and cleared my throat.

Rosa smiled and left Emma's room, probably to give me privacy. I pushed the call button and put the phone up to my ear.

"Hello?"

"Mom?"

"Of course. You were expecting someone else?"

"Ha ha." I rolled my eyes. "Mom, I'm at Emma's. May I stay here for dinner tonight?"

"Uh, no. Actually, I was about to call you. You need to come home in an hour. I'm still at school, finishing up semester report cards."

"Can Emma eat dinner with us, then?"

"Not tonight, sweetie."

"Why not?"

"Because I think we need some family time. Bye, V. I'll see you in an hour."

I clicked "end call" and slid my phone back into my pocket without saying bye.

"What did she say?" Emma asked.

"She said we need 'family time,' whatever that means."

"She probably just wants to spend time with you and Scotty. My mom does that, too. Moms are funny that way, wanting to spend time with their kids." Emma laughed but stopped when she saw my unsmiling face. "Gee, tough room."

"I don't buy it. Mom pretty much never says no to me. You know that. She loves you and always tells you how welcome you are at our house 'any time.' Something else is going on with her. She acted strange on the phone just now. Well, strange for her."

"I think you're reading too much into it. She's probably just trying to get her work wrapped up so she can get out of there and enjoy Christmas break."

"I don't know . . . but I hope you're right."

Exactly one hour later . . .

I walked through the front door, and Mom greeted me with, "Do you have to go to the bathroom?"

"No. What kind of a hello is that?"

Mom giggled, her green eyes sparkling with mischief. "Get in the car, V. We're going somewhere."

"For dinner?"

"Something like that."

"Where are we going?"

"It's a surprise."

"Why? What's going on?"

"V, just get in the car," Dad said. "Stop giving your mom a hard time."

"I'm not giving Mom a hard t—" I stopped myself.

Scotty ran up to me with Lucky in his arms. "We're going camping, and we get to bring Lucky!"

"Camping?! What the heck?"

"You weren't supposed to tell her yet, sweetie," Mom said to Scotty with a wink.

"Oops, sorry, Mommy."

"Camping? In the winter? Seriously?" I couldn't believe what I was hearing.

"Don't be so dramatic," Mom said. "It's not like it snows in southern California."

"But —"

"All will be revealed in the car. We've got to leave now if we're going to get there in time. Come on."

"And my clothes?"

"Packed."

"Mom!"

"Car." She pointed toward the door.

At that point, I knew better than to keep arguing with her. I sighed and walked through the door, climbing into the back seat of our forest green Subaru Outback with Scotty and Lucky. *Yay, family trip. Lucky me.*

The drive to Joshua Tree National Park took two hours. We stopped at In-N-Out for a quick drive-thru dinner. Lucky got a burger, too—pup patty.

I tried not to grumble too much but really had no idea why the impromptu vacation, and why my parents didn't tell me about it until literally five minutes before we left. I stared out the back window, arms folded across my chest, earbuds in, listening to Taylor Swift. Not that I was much of a Swiftie, but

Emma was. Emma adored everything about Taylor Swift, and I adored pretty much everything about Emma. Therefore, I was a fan by default. But my musical taste was kind of all over the place, depending on my mood. It ranged as diverse as hip hop to classical.

After twenty minutes or so of my brooding silence, I couldn't stand it anymore. I popped out an earbud and asked, "So now are you going to tell me where we're going—and why?"

"You owe me ten bucks," Dad said to Mom.

"The silence couldn't last forever, could it?" Mom replied.

"What? You guys made a bet on me? What kind of sick and twisted parents are you?" I snuck a peek at Scotty to make sure he didn't just hear me call our parents "sick and twisted." He was immersed in a Disney movie on his iPad, clutching Lucky's soft fur next to him like a security blanket.

Mom laughed. "The kind who don't plan ahead. The kind who go on spontaneous family vacations because 'why not?' Don't read too much into it, sweetheart. There's really nothing to be upset about. We didn't conspire against you. A fellow teacher at work rented a house at Joshua Tree over the holidays but had to back out at the last minute. Instead of trying to get a refund, he asked around first to see if anyone wanted it. Your dad jumped at it and sealed the deal before telling anyone— including me. I found out about ten minutes before you called from Emma's. Personally, I love Dad's unplanned surprises."

Dad squeezed her knee, and they beamed at each other. *Ew.*

A Joshua tree is a bizarrely-shaped tree that looks like how I would imagine it would look if a palm tree and a cactus plant had a baby. They're strange and barren looking, but also kind of beautiful in their own way. They grow in the Mojave Desert, and apparently, they are quite the tourist attraction.

"We're camping in the desert in *December*?" I couldn't keep the disdain out of my voice.

"No, silly," Scotty piped up. "We're staying in a house!"

"Oh, right. I stand corrected. But doesn't it get cold in the desert?"

"Not that cold," Dad said. "I think the lowest it gets is about forty degrees, at night."

"Will it snow?" Scotty asked. "Like when we went on that trip to Oregon, in the mountains? That was so cool! Can we have snow for Christmas again? Please?"

"I don't think so, li'l man," Dad said. "It has to be really, really cold for it to snow."

"Oh. Sorry, Lucky, I guess you don't get to see your first snow yet." Scotty patted Lucky on the head, and Lucky looked up at him as though hanging on his every word.

We rode in silence for a bit, and Scotty and I both nodded off.

I startled awake to Mom's voice, shouting, "We're here!"

Dad eased the car down the long, windy driveway toward a plain, ranch-style house. Nothing special—it was a rental after all. But it was the closest to the park we could get.

It was after 7:30 by the time we unloaded the car and put dibs on our rooms. Scotty and I couldn't wait to get back outside and gaze at the stars. After all, we were in the middle of nowhere . . . near a desert. Except for the stars, it was pitch black all around us.

We bundled up in coats, hats, and scarves, and headed for the door.

"Take this blanket to lay on," Mom called out, handing me a thick quilt and a flashlight.

"Good idea, thanks." I gave her a quick hug, my form of apology for giving her attitude earlier.

"Come on, V! Let's count the stars!" Scotty ran out to the front yard, spinning in circles with his head tilted so far back he was either going to do a backbend or fall over and land on his head.

"Slow down, Scotty. You're gonna get dizzy and fall."

"No, I'm not. Watch this—" His words cut off as he hit the dirt, knocking the wind out of him.

I threw the blanket down and aimed the flashlight at him. He lay still in the yard, which consisted of sagebrush, a few cactus plants, tumbleweeds, and dirt. Or maybe it was sand? We were in the desert after all.

I ran over to him, shining the flashlight in his face. "Are you okay?"

He covered his eyes with his hands, squinting. "V, turn it off! I'm looking at the stars!"

I breathed a sigh of relief, spread out the blanket, and invited him to lie next to me on the warm blanket instead of the cold sand-dirt. He took me up on it.

"The stars sure are bright tonight," I said, admiring the celestial view and clear desert skies.

"Yeah, and there's millions and millions of them," Scotty marveled. "What do you want Santa to bring you for Christmas?"

So much for a philosophical discussion about astronomy or the meaning of life. But then again, what did I expect from a seven-year-old? "A new car," I said.

"Wow, that's a big present! How will Santa fit it on his sleigh?"

"He won't. A car isn't in Santa's budget this year."

"What's a budget?"

"He can't afford it."

"Oh." Scotty was silent for a bit. Then he asked, "What does your new car look like?"

I beamed, happily relaying the details of the beautiful red sports car of my dreams. I closed my eyes and pictured myself posing next to it. I described the beach where it's parked on the sand and my yellow and white polka dot sundress, the closest thing I owned to dressing up. The purple canopy of bright stars shining down on me, to match the bright smile on my beaming face.

"V, tell me the story," he interrupted.

"But I'm telling you about my car."

"I don't want to hear about your car anymore. Tell me *the* story."

"That's Mom's story."

"Yeah, but you could tell it."

"No, I can't. I don't remember it well enough. Besides, you can read now. You should write it down so you can read it whenever you want."

"Silly, I can't write it down. It's in Mommy's head."

"Oh."

"Is Mommy's cancer made of glass? Will she break like the glass stars in her story?"

"No, of course not. Her cancer is gone, remember?"

"But what if she gets sick again?"

"She's not going to get sick again."

"But what if she does?"

Crap. He was right. What if Mom got sick again and

wouldn't be able to tell him the bedtime story anymore? Or if she forgot it? A slow smile crept over my face as I gazed up at the stars. I had an idea for the perfect Christmas present for Scotty.

As Mom told Scotty the story at his bedtime that night, the same story she'd been telling him nearly every night for almost two years, I secretly recorded it with the voice recorder on my phone. The next morning, I transcribed it by typing it all out on Google Docs on my phone. Luckily, the house we were renting had a computer and a printer for guest use. I was able to AirPrint out the story. But I didn't want to staple it together because Scotty might poke himself with the staple. I also needed something sturdier so the paper wouldn't rip or fall apart.

As we were out and about that day, I asked Dad to stop at a drugstore. I found a report binder I could use for Scotty's story. *Perfect.* Later, I made a cover for it and wrapped it up, hiding it in my bag until Christmas morning.

While we played tourists and shopped for trinkets and treasures, Scotty and I saw some beautiful amethyst crystals and stones at a store Mom and Dad wanted to stop at. The sign next to the amethysts said the stones had healing powers. I read it out loud to Scotty, "A remarkable healing stone, removing pain and tension while bringing energy and a sense of well-being to the mind and body. The amethyst crystal calms and soothes, assisting the transmission of neural signals through the brain."

"Is it magic?" Scotty asked.

"I don't know, maybe. But it can't hurt. Maybe it can help keep Mom healthy, by bringing her body good energy. Shall we get it for her, for Christmas?"

"Yeah! That's a great present! Let's get this one." He pointed at a beautiful large crystal geode.

"Oh, sorry buddy, that's way out of my price range. It's also too big and heavy. Let's get her something she can keep on her nightstand, so it's near her when she sleeps."

"Oh yeah, good idea. How about that one?" He pointed toward a much smaller crystal egg.

"Perfect. In fact, how about if I get you one, too, for good luck? It'll keep the worries away."

"Yes! Thank you, V! Can I have this one?" He pointed to a small stone. "It's little enough to fit in my pocket."

"Excellent selection."

"Do you want one, too? I can get it for you for your Christmas present."

"Thank you, Scotty. That's so thoughtful of you." I picked out a small keychain. "How about this one?"

"Okay, but I don't have any money. Can I pay you back?"

"Sure." I patted him on the head, and we walked up to the cashier to buy the magical gifts with healing powers.

Our week at Joshua Tree flew by. Even though I wasn't asked—was, in fact, forced to go—wasn't allowed a say, vote, or opinion, and wasn't allowed to bring Emma, I had a decent time reconnecting with my family. Okay, I'll admit it was better than decent, fun even, but I was anxious to get back and get my driver's permit with Emma. We'd been texting each other all week.

Emma wanted to get us an appointment for December 24th, but that was Christmas Eve and a Saturday, and the Department of Motor Vehicles (DMV) was closed. Then because of Christmas, they didn't open again till Tuesday. *Sigh.* Luckily, she got us in for Tuesday morning at 8:30. December 27th couldn't get here fast enough.

For me, there's just something about that milestone, that rite of passage that would get me one step closer to a sense of freedom and independence. Someday, I would have my own car and be able to go wherever, whenever I want. But until then, I had to try to practice patience and enjoy this moment, this time with my family, hiking the rocky terrain of this strangely beautiful desert wilderness with my little brother.

My phone chimed. Thinking it was Emma, I pulled the phone out of my pocket and glanced at the texts from Crash.

CRASH

Are you dying of thirst in the desert?

Wait, you can't text back because you're in a remote village of sand people. And there's no electricity or phone chargers.

Your phone must have died.

Hope you come back to civilization soon.

I rolled my eyes and shoved my phone back into my pocket. Crash had been texting me all week, sending me stupid puns and jokes. I didn't reply, not even a laugh emoji. When I told Emma and Brylee about it, Brylee said if I didn't want to encourage him that I should just ghost him and he'd stop. *Nope, this guy can't take a hint. Why won't he just go away? We're not even friends. But . . . he is kinda cute. NO! I'm not going there. I can't.*

"V! Get over here, quick! I think I see a rattlesnake!" Scotty screamed.

"Scotty, don't move! Where is it? Ohmygosh, I forgot what you do when you see a rattlesnake! Is it hold still like a statue or run as fast as you can? Oh no! Help!" My breathing came in short, ragged breaths as I tried not to panic. I had to get to Scotty before *he* panicked. *Oh crap! Please, no, not on my watch. Please don't let my brother get bitten by a rattlesnake. Please, please, please.* I wiped my sweaty palms on my jeans and tried to take a deep, calming breath. *What would Veronica do?*

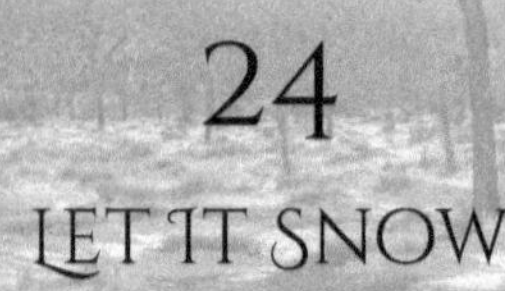

24

LET IT SNOW

As it turned out, the snake was just as scared of us as we were of it. I slowly inched my way over to Scotty with my finger over my lips, cautioning him to be quiet. I bent down and picked up Lucky, grateful that he hadn't barked —or worse, chased the snake, trying to make friends with it. As far as I could tell, he hadn't even seen it. Luckily for Lucky! We watched the snake slither away, in the opposite direction from where we were, until it was out of sight and behind a big rock.

Needless to say, I wasn't about to wait for the snake to make another appearance. I held on to Lucky in my left arm, grabbed Scotty's hand with my right hand, and walked as fast as I could, without dragging Scotty along, back to our parents. I quickly told them about the snake, and we didn't waste any time getting out of there. I'd seen enough nature to last a good, long while, and I was all too happy Mom gave us an out without rousing Scotty's anxiety.

"Let's give the snake some peace and quiet. I think it must be his nap time. Who wants to head back to the cabin for some hot cocoa?"

"Me! I do!" Scotty chimed in.

Thank you, Mom!

Early Christmas morning ...

"It's snowing!" Scotty shouted near me.

I rolled over to catch more Z's.

"V, wake up! My Christmas wish came true! It's snowing!" Scotty and Lucky both jumped on me. Lucky licked my face.

No sleeping through this. I sighed. "All right, I'm awake. Geesh." I sat up and rubbed the sleep from my eyes.

"Grouchy bear! Wanna play in the snow?"

"It doesn't snow in the desert."

"Uh-huh! Look outside!"

"What time is it?"

"I don't know. It's Christmastime! Time to get up!"

"Right. Okay. Be right there, squirt."

"I'm not a squirt! I told you to stop calling me that!"

"Sure thing, not-a-squirt."

"V!" Scotty wailed, pummeling his fists into my gut.

"Oof." The air whooshed out of me all at once. I pinned his hands away, contemplating my next move.

"What's all the commotion in here, li'l man?" Dad walked in and scooped up Scotty. "How about we give your sister a couple minutes to wake up and get dressed, huh?" He winked at me and walked back out with Scotty in his arms, giggling, and Lucky at his heels. *My hero.*

I set my feet upon the cold, ceramic tiles, feeling a slight chill. I stood up, stretched, and sauntered over to the window. Sure enough, there was a smattering of snow on the ground and tiny flakes slowly falling. Obviously, it wasn't nearly enough to "play in," but it was definitely snowing. The disparity between the soft, white snowflakes and the starkness of the desert was a sight to behold. *Snow in the desert? Imagine that. Scotty got his wish after all.*

WE OPENED OUR STOCKINGS, ate yummy chocolate chip pancakes with candy canes in our cocoa for breakfast, cleaned up the kitchen, and opened our presents. Everyone loved their gifts, and it gave me a warm feeling inside to see my family so happy. This was the first time I could remember being truly happy since before Emma was kidnapped . . . since before Mom was diagnosed with cancer. Emma was back, we were best friends again, and my mom's cancer was in remission. It didn't matter what other presents I got this year; I had everything I wanted. Well, almost. *I still want my dream car!*

Since I mentioned the C word, Mom got two more graphic T-shirts from Rebecca Nichols, her best friend and my freshman English teacher, that said, "Redheads are sunshine mixed with a little hurricane" and "This ain't my first rodeo." By now, Mom had collected quite an assortment of colorful sayings and graphic tees with attitude. And of course, she had many and varied versions of "F*** cancer" T-shirts given to her by former students and adoring fans. My mom was not to be messed with.

But the best part about Christmas morning for me? Watching Scotty open the story I had typed and printed out for him and seeing the realization and awe on his face when he figured out what it was. He held up his beloved, "The Legend of the Glass Stars," story for all to see, beaming. "Thank you, V! Will you read it to me?"

I opened my mouth to reply when Mom intercepted. "Actually, sweetie, why don't you read the story to us? Show Daddy and V what a good reader you are now. Remember to read loud and clear, like we practiced."

I shot Mom a look and mouthed, "Practiced?"

"Scotty's teacher is working with their class on read-alouds. So we've been practicing reading out loud lately, and Scotty is a very good reader. Isn't that right, sweetie?" She winked at Scotty and patted the couch next to her.

Scotty picked up the story, walked over to the couch, and plopped down next to Mom. He cleared his throat, took two big breaths, and began to read.

25

"THE LEGEND OF THE GLASS STARS"

Many moons ago, long before people inhabited Earth, animals reigned over the lands. Among them lived an enormous, giant bird. According to the Native American legends, this giant bird, who resembled an eagle, but was much, much bigger, was called Thunderbird—or Skyamsen, as he is known in some tribes.

Thunderbird was a Spirit God. He had a wingspan of twenty-five feet and talons strong enough to pick up and carry off a whale. It was said that he controlled the weather.

By flapping his wings, he made thunder and wind. The tears from his eyes made the rain. And from his beak, he shot powerful lightning bolts across the skies.

The symbol for Thunderbird's lightning bolt is a simple zigzag that can still be seen in many pottery and art designs today.

Thunderbird flew back and forth all across the lands, making sure the plants and animals had fresh water whenever they needed it. He filled the lakes and streams with his tears of rain; he formed new rivers and paths with his strong winds.

When the animals fought each other or provoked Thunderbird, he simply flapped his mighty wings and the deafening thunderclaps rolled out wherever he wanted them to, sending the animals sprinting away in fright. If it was dark, he lit up the sky with his lightning.

One day, bored with merely controlling the weather, Thunderbird wanted to create something extraordinary. He thought and thought about what he could make. By nightfall, as he observed the sky and the stars all around him, he noticed how tiny they were. They seemed inconsequential and unimpressive to him. Some of the stars were very dim, just faintly shining.

"Ha. I can do better than that!" he shouted out to the very

stars themselves. You see, Thunderbird spent most of his days and nights alone. Too busy and important to play with the other animals, Thunderbird had never made any friends.

Way up in the sky, far from our planet, it was always night-time—and the stars were always shining. Thunderbird flew among the stars and found a small smattering of stardust that had been left by a passing supernova. The dust looked just like the grains of sand we see on the beach. He knew that when sand gets hot enough, it turns to glass.

Suddenly, he had an idea for his extraordinary creation. He gathered up all of his strength, squeezed his eyes shut tight, and concentrated his energy on making his beak as hot as he possibly could. Then he shot a lightning bolt out of his beak at the stardust. Instantly, a giant glass star formed before him.

The newly formed glass star shone brighter than all the other stars in the galaxy. It had been formed from a fire hotter than molten lava—it was the prettiest and most radiant star in the night sky.

Thunderbird was very pleased with himself.

Each night, he searched for more stardust and formed more and more glass stars so he could lovingly spread them out all over the sky for all of creation to see. He would have kept on making them for hundreds of thousands of years; they were so beautiful he couldn't help himself.

But one night, he carelessly kicked a glass star with his massive talon. It broke, shattering into a million pieces and scattering into oblivion. Thunderbird realized that his glass stars were fragile, simply because they were made of glass.

This saddened him greatly. With a heavy heart, Thunderbird carefully gathered up all of his precious glass stars. Every single star that he had made and spread throughout the galaxy, he retrieved, one by one.

Finally, he clustered them all close together to form a beautiful, giant spiral. This cluster of billions of stars he created is what we now call the Milky Way. Thunderbird believed that if his delicate stars were all in one place, he could protect them and keep them safe.

Every now and then, his glass stars drifted away, out of the safe zone. When that happened, they broke, and Thunderbird mourned them. But sometimes, he was fast enough to find and catch them. He brought those stars back to the safety of the giant spiral, where they stayed for hundreds of thousands of years.

To this day, according to the legend, if you watch the night sky very closely, you can still see Thunderbird tearing through it and clutching a beloved glass star in his mighty talons. He soars through the night skies to lovingly put the glass star back into the Milky Way, where he can watch over and protect it for all eternity.

The End

SCOTTY READ the entire story in a strong, clear voice, stumbling occasionally over a few big words. I glanced at my parents as he read and saw the tears in Mom's eyes. When he finished, we all clapped and cheered.

"Well done, li'l man!" Dad said, clapping and whistling. "You are a most excellent reader."

By this time, the tears in Mom's eyes had toppled over and were cascading down her cheeks. She wiped at them and sniffled, then said, "My sweet Scotty, you can read to me any day." She hugged him tight until he squirmed and asked her to let him go.

Resisting the urge to tear up myself, I sucked it up and said, "Good job, squirt."

"V! Stop calling me squirt!" Scotty protested. He leaped off the couch and pummeled my stomach with his little fists. I counter-attacked by reaching down and tickling his ribs. He dissolved into fits of giggly laughter, that beautiful, melodic sound of a happy child without a care in the world. *Best. Christmas. Ever.*

26

96 PERCENT!

We drove home on Christmas day after our early supper around three o'clock. We'd feasted on Honey Baked Ham with all the trimmings, and our bellies were full. Scotty and I were primed for sleeping all the way home. There's nothing like a cozy nap in the car to make the ride home go faster. We wanted to get back and spend time with our friends. Scotty couldn't wait to show Alex his story, still amazed that I was able to type it just as Mom had always told it, and I wanted to start studying for the driver's permit test with Emma. I'd read the California Driver's Manual once, sort of. I definitely needed to go through it a few more times, or there's no way I was going to pass this test.

There was no one on the roads when we left. Another good reason to leave early, Mom had said. Who drives home from a trip on Christmas day? We do! Besides, Mom and Dad knew better than to try to keep us all cooped up together in the desert much longer. It had been a fun week, and I think Mom wanted to end the trip on a good note, before Scotty and I decided to quarrel about something stupid and ruin it. By the time we packed up and left, the inch of snow that had been on the ground that morning had melted away into a nice memory that Scotty and I would always cherish. And I had the pictures of Scotty and Lucky with their tongues stretched out, trying to taste snowflakes, to prove it.

As soon as we got home, I asked if I could go to Emma's. I would have texted her sooner as a heads-up, but like I said, I'd slept the entire drive home. After texting Emma that I was on my way, I checked my phone and saw more messages from Crash.

CRASH

How was your Christmas?

Was Santa good to you this year or did you get a lump of coal in your stocking? Hahahaha

Again, I didn't reply. *What is wrong with this guy? He really needs to get a clue.*

MOM DROPPED Emma and me off at the DMV at 8:20 a.m. Tuesday morning. We'd made up flashcards and studied all day Monday, so we both felt prepared. The written test was composed of forty-six multiple choice questions. I felt confident about most of my answers as I circled my choices. You had to get an 83 percent to pass, which meant I could get eight wrong. I knew that if I missed a few I'd be okay.

Emma and I finished our tests at about the same time. Fortunately, they graded the tests right there on the spot and gave us our scores with the correct answers of the ones we missed. We both passed! We were so excited! Emma missed three, and I only missed two! I got a 96 percent! *Oh yeah! Look out, world, V is driving!*

The DMV lady gave us a piece of paper, announcing we could drive and that our brand-new driver's permits would be delivered via mail in about ten days. Meanwhile, they said we had to keep the paper with us every time we drove. I quickly sent Mom a text that it was over, and she said she'd meet us out front in ten minutes.

We could finally drive! Of course, we needed an adult to ride with us, but at least we were that much closer to our goal. Our legal papers stating we could drive in hand, we met Mom at the curb, told her the good news, and I promptly asked, "Can I drive home?"

"Oh no, I'm not ready for that yet," Mom said.

"If not now, then when?" I pouted.

"How about if your dad takes you out a couple times first, okay? He's much more even-keeled and patient. I'm afraid I'm not capable of sitting in the passenger seat next to my baby girl while she drives me around. You're growing up entirely too fast, and I'm just not ready."

"Oh Mom." I rolled my eyes and got in the back seat next to Emma. "Fine, then you can be our chauffeur instead."

"Fine by me." She turned up the radio, and we all laughed.

Wednesday was my parents' seventeenth anniversary. They said they wanted a "kid-free" celebration, so Scotty spent the night at Alex's and I spent the night at Emma's. It had been so long since I last stayed at Emma's. Her mom made us popcorn and cocoa, and we stayed up late, watching scary movies. It was so fun just to hang out with Emma with no homework, no agenda, and no cares. I blocked out anything bad so I could stay in my happy bubble. If only I could have stayed there forever. I just wanted to enjoy the rest of the school year with Emma, in peace. No more detective stuff, no more sticking my neck out; just the normal status quo. I'd had enough drama the last year-and-a-half to last a lifetime.

EMMA, Brylee, and I spent New Year's Eve together at Brylee's house. After the last high school party we'd gone to together, where Brylee drank too much and passed out, and I almost got 'date raped,' as Emma kept insisting, none of us wanted to go anywhere near another party. I requested an old-fashioned 'girls only' sleepover, and Brylee and Emma agreed. And surprisingly, Brylee wanted to have the sleepover at her house.

We gave each other manis and pedis with Brylee's own nail station. She lived in a mansion and had an enormous bedroom with her own bathroom. She even had servants! I knew she was rich, but she never talked about it, at least not to me. This was the first time I'd been inside her house. Apparently, her parents were very private. They didn't have people over very often.

I met her mom and stepdad briefly. They seemed nice. They were all dressed up and headed out to a nice restaurant with friends of theirs. Brylee's two younger sisters poked their heads in her room a couple times, but she yelled at them to get out and the maid shooed them away.

For the most part, it was a fun night, and I enjoyed hanging out with them. Except for the hour or so Brylee cried about her breakup with Santi, and Emma and I had to cheer her up, it was a great New Year's Eve. *Happy New Year!*

January 3rd

SEEING Crash in Computer class first period was uncomfortably awkward, to say the least. He tried to get my attention, but I pretended I didn't see him. I stared intently at the computer monitor in front of me, eyes riveted on the blinking cursor. You'd think I was watching a thriller on Netflix. When the bell rang, I dashed out the door as fast as I could, not daring to look back.

Second period English wasn't much better. Miss Torres assigned a four-paragraph, persuasive, in-class essay based on a quote by the motivational speaker, Dr. Wayne Dyer (whom I'd never heard of before). She said we had the class period to decide if we believed the statement to be true or false, and then write a persuasive essay to convince our audience of our stance.

It was due at the end of class; we had fifty minutes. I groaned because I was terrible at in-class essays. I hated writing with a literal time bomb ticking away. The pressure was unbearable.

I was a slow writer. It took me a while to gather my thoughts, at least in a way where I could write coherent sentences, come up with a thesis statement, and follow paragraph and essay structure. Besides, having an English teacher for a mom didn't help. You'd think it would, but it didn't. I had grown accustomed to her proofreading my essays for me. I guess you could say she was my crutch; I leaned on her to help me with my homework. She knew exactly how to get me out of a writing jam when I got stuck. With her tips, essay writing became easy for me. But only in the moment, if that makes sense. In class, I felt stupid and couldn't remember any of Mom's useful tips, like I just couldn't get my brain to think right.

Miss Torres pulled up the projector screen to reveal the quote on the whiteboard and told us to begin writing. I blinked. I slowly read the words again. My stomach churned. Was this my teacher's idea of a personal attack? What the heck? Suddenly, I felt under a spotlight, or maybe a microscope. The walls closed in. Was everyone staring at me? My name might as well have been written on the board, too. It was so obvious to me that this was directed at me. The quote? Yeah, it's for me.

When given the choice between being right or being kind, choose kind.

— DR. WAYNE W. DYER

Miss Torres asked us to look at both sides of everything these days—the good and the bad, the villain's point of view, being in someone else's shoes, et cetera. It was as if that little pep talk she had given me the first week of school grew inside her head and became a whole two-week lecture targeted at me. *"Class, for the next two weeks we're going to study ways to make V a nicer, kinder person. She's currently angry with herself, and we need to teach her forgiveness, for herself and others."*

I glared down at my paper and started writing gibberish. But the truth was, I *had* changed since my talk with Miss Torres that first week of school. I had everything I wanted now. My world was good. I had Emma and Brylee and my family. Even Suzie and I were friends again since she had helped me adopt Lucky. I was happy. I smiled more. I didn't argue as much.

But had I forgiven myself? A conversation began in my head with my conscience. I couldn't get her to shut up.

Me: *What is there to forgive? I haven't done anything wrong.*

Myself: *But you're mean to Crash.*

Me: *No, I'm not. He just wants more than I can give him right now. I'm not interested in him like that. Whatever, leave me alone. I'm doing the best I can.*

Myself: *What about Pedro?*

Me: *What about him?*

Myself: *You're just going to let him continue to harass and terrorize people? What about what he's doing to Mr. C?*

Me: *Oh, Mr. C. Emma and I have Driver's Ed class after school today.*

Myself: *That's not the point.*

Me: *I don't care about Pedro and his stupid gang. I can't. I have to think of the safety of my friends and family. Don't I?*

Myself: *How is turning your back on Mr. C being kind?*

Me: *Shut up. This stupid essay! I don't want to think about any of this right now.*

I tore a sheet of paper out of my notebook and crumpled it up into a little ball.

"What's the matter, V? Are you all right?" Miss Torres stood beside my desk, looking down at me.

"Yeah, I'm fine."

"I've been meaning to check in with you since our talk last semester. How are things going?"

"You're asking me that now?" I glanced around the room at my classmates to see who noticed, but they were focused on their own essays.

"Well, yes." Miss Torres kneeled down, eye level with me, and lowered her voice. "I've noticed your demeanor has improved, and I was wondering if you've figured it out."

"Figured what out?"

She leaned in closer and whispered, "How to forgive yourself." She smiled as she stood up, smoothed down her skirt, and walked over to her desk without waiting for my answer.

Believe it or not, that gave me the push I needed. Like my brain jump-started and was working again. I wrote a solid essay, I thought, on the merits of kindness and how being kind truly was better than being right. I thought of all the times I'd corrected someone or when I hadn't bitten my tongue but definitely should've. I'd seen the embarrassment and hurt in their eyes at being called out. I knew my sarcasm sometimes hurt others, especially Emma, who was always so sweet. Why was I like that? Sarcasm just came so naturally for me. It usually rolled out of my mouth before I had a chance to think whether I should say it or not. And look where it had gotten me. I'd been sent to the principal's office numerous times last year for arguing with teachers, picking fights with classmates during class, and having "anger issues." My sharp tongue prevented me from getting to know Brylee sooner, and nearly cost me my friendship with Emma. It had gotten me sent to my room more than once when I'd been disrespectful to my parents or provoked Scotty. I blamed others for my actions, but the truth was, I was so afraid of losing the people I cared about that I'd nearly pushed them away anyway. My lack of kindness when Emma and Brylee were missing had left me alone and friendless. Yes, it was better to be kind. It reminded me of that old saying my third grade teacher used to say, "If you don't have anything nice to say, don't say anything at all."

I turned in my essay seconds before the bell rang, satisfied with what I'd written. As I walked down the hall toward my locker, I felt a hand on my shoulder. Thinking it was Emma, I turned around with a broad smile, only to find Crash's eyes fixed on mine. My smile turned into a frown.

"We need to talk," he said.

"Crash, I don't think—"

"Why did you ghost me all break?" he interrupted. "I'm hurt. I thought we were friends."

"Why? Because we had a couple driving lessons together?"

"Well, yeah. I'm the one who told you about Dan's Driving Instruction. Besides, I thought—"

"Crash, I don't owe you a thing. Why can't you just leave me alone?"

"Is . . . is that what you really want?"

"Yes, it is. Please, just pretend we never met. Okay?" I saw the anguish in his eyes and quickly looked away. *So much for being kind.* "I'm sorry. I have to go." I turned and walked away. I needed a reason *not* to like him. I didn't have room in my circle for anyone else right now.

I RAN into Suzie in the hallway during lunch. And by "ran into," I mean I stalked her until I found her walking toward the library. "Hey, Suzie, how are you?"

"Oh, hey, V. How's your puppy doing?"

"Lucky's doing great. Thank you again for helping my family adopt him. He goes everywhere, except to school, with Scotty. They're inseparable."

"Awesome. I'm so glad it worked out." Suzie smiled.

"Uh, you're still an office aide, right?"

She crossed her arms, suddenly guarded. "Yeah, why?"

I ignored the sudden icy tone in her voice and went for the ask. "Will you get Crash—I mean, Zack's student file for me?"

"What? No way. I could get in a lot of trouble for that. But, why do you want it? Do you like him or something?"

"Ew. No, of course not!"

"If you're so curious about him, why don't you just ask him yourself? You have ways of getting stuff out of people, V. I can't help you."

"But I need dirt on him. Like, why did he really transfer here? Did he ever get in trouble at his old school? Stuff he's not going to freely tell me."

"I'm going to hate myself for asking this, but why do you need dirt on him?"

"Because he won't leave me alone. He constantly texts me and won't take a hint. He annoys the heck out of me. I need leverage in case I have to use it to get him to go away."

"Seriously? Just tell him you're not interested."

"I did. It didn't work. The guy won't take no for an answer."

"Then ignore him."

"I tried that, too."

"Whatever."

"Does that mean you'll do it?"

She rolled her eyes. "Sure, I guess. I know a bit about guys who won't leave you alone. But you owe me."

I blinked, surprised she actually agreed since she was such a strict rule follower. "Absolutely! You got it, anything you need."

"Right."

"Really, anything."

28

CORY

Emma and I met up at my locker after school, then we walked over to the visitor's parking area to wait for our first driving lesson with Dan. Since I'd already had two ride-along lessons, I recognized the ugly green Ford Fiesta pull into campus and head toward us. I frowned when I saw someone I didn't recognize behind the wheel.

"Well hello again, Victoria! Long time, no see," Mr. C said as he got out of the car. "And who do we have here?"

"Hi, Mr. C. My name is Violet, remember? Actually, please call me V. This is my friend Emma. I told you about her when I signed up to take your course again after having to drop out last fall. I paid our deposits online, on your website."

"Oh yes, of course. I remember now. Sorry about that, V. Won't happen again. Hello, Emma. So lovely to meet you."

"You, too?" Emma said, unsure what to think of this guy.

"He's a bit quirky, but you'll get used to him. He's harmless," I whispered.

"Go ahead and get in the back, girls. I have another student who needs to finish the course today."

"Wait, I don't understand," I said. "You said it would just be Emma and me. If we split our time with someone else, won't we have to log extra hours?"

"Not at all. Since you already have four hours in, you're actually ahead of the game, V. Now get in, please. Time's a-wasting." He smiled a little too broad and opened the back door for us.

Emma and I exchanged a look. I shrugged. We climbed in the car and fastened our seat belts. The student driver had a short crew cut of thick black hair, slightly wavy on top. His skin was medium-brown, and his big brown eyes stared intently at me in the rearview mirror for a split second longer than they should before he pulled out of the lot and drove us away from the school. It was unsettling. Something about his gaze reminded me of someone. I tried to shake it off.

"Okay, Cory. Take a left here and get on the freeway. I want to see if your merging has improved since I asked you to practice more with your parents last week."

"Cory?" Emma and I both mouthed at each other at the same time. Brylee's younger brother, Corbyn, went by Cory. But he was away at an all-boys boarding school. *Wasn't he? Is he back? Could this be him?* Since neither Emma nor I had ever met him, and Brylee rarely talked about him, we couldn't be sure.

But why would he take Dan's driving course? And at the same time as Emma and me? This was way too weird to be a coincidence. Suddenly, my mind leaped to Pedro. No, I couldn't go there. It was just a coincidence, nothing more. It probably wasn't even Brylee's brother. Here I was, being paranoid for nothing. *I really gotta lay off the detective shows!*

"Sure thing, Mr. C," Cory said. He glanced at me in the rearview mirror again and smiled. A chill rose up my spine.

After driving around for about an hour, Mr. C told Cory to

pull into Milo's. A sinking feeling in my gut made me want to bolt out of that car right then. *Oh no, not this again. Mr. C must still be involved with Pedro's gang. I can't believe they're using the same convenience store parking lot as their exchange/drop-off. How stupid can they get?*

I sat in stunned silence. But I had to know if this was Brylee's brother. I had to know if he was involved. I had to know if Pedro was behind this.

Mr. C told us to go in and get ourselves a snack, just like before, while he filled up the car at the gas station down the street. He said he'd be right back. *Here we go again.*

Emma said she had to use the restroom and went inside. Cory said he had to make a phone call and walked around the corner. I stood in front of the glass doors, wondering if I should pursue this or let it go. After a moment's hesitation, I walked around the corner to ask Cory outright if he was Brylee's brother. *Rip the Band-Aid off clean, no more games.*

I cleared the corner and spotted the familiar dumpsters about halfway down the alley, where Pedro had threatened me nearly four months ago. I couldn't see further down because the dumpsters obstructed my view. Maybe that's why they still used this spot. It was behind a store, in an alley, and fairly concealed. I didn't see Cory anywhere, so I crept up to the dumpsters and snuck a peek around the side.

Sure enough, there was Mr. C's car backed up to another car, trunks open, and being loaded up by a couple guys I didn't recognize. *New recruits?* At least I didn't see Santi. By the front of the other car I saw Pedro and Cory talking. My heart sank. If this really was Brylee's little brother, I had a feeling we were all in trouble. I couldn't hear what they were saying, and I wasn't any good at reading lips. I decided to get out of there before I got caught, reliving what happened the last time I did this.

I went back inside the store and bought a Twix candy bar while waiting for Emma. She came out of the restroom, cheeks flushed and right hand over her lower abdomen.

"Cramps?" I asked, knowingly.

"Yep, the worst," she said. "I just want to crawl into a ball and take a long nap till they go away."

"I hear ya. At least your first driving lesson should help take your mind off it."

"Great, don't remind me."

"Nervous?"

"After riding in a car with you? Terrified!"

We both laughed and walked outside to find Mr. C and Cory waiting for us. "Who wants to go next? V? Emma?"

We looked at each other, each one pointing to the other. Finally, Emma said, "Okay, fine. Let's get this over with. I'll go next, Mr. C."

"Wonderful! Do you have any behind-the-wheel experience, Emma?"

"Nope."

"This should be fun," Cory muttered under his breath.

We all got in the car. Mr. C went over the basics of driving with Emma and coaxed her out of the parking lot. I leaned over to Cory in the back seat next to me and said, "Does Brylee know?"

Shock and fear passed over his face for the briefest second before he composed himself, but I saw it. It wouldn't matter what he said next. I knew all I needed to know.

"EMMA, we have to tell Brylee. You know how hurt she was when I didn't tell her about Santi. We have to tell her about Cory, and we have to tell her now."

Emma saw the look in my eyes and knew there was no arguing with me. "Okay, I'll text her and ask her to meet us at the rec center."

"The rec center? Why would we meet her there?"

"Because, I told my mom I'd check it out after my driving class today. She wants me to do volunteer work. She said it looks good on college applications. I'm going to volunteer at the community center or the senior center. I haven't decided which yet. As long as the hours are flexible and don't compete with soccer, I'll do it."

"I'll get Dad to drive us over."

"WHAT'S SO important you made me drive over here and miss *The Walking Dead*?" Brylee asked as she sauntered up to us in flannel PJ bottoms, a baggy T-shirt, and UGG boots.

"I see you dressed up for us," I said.

"Shut up. What's this all about? I really just want to get back home and relax. Not feeling super social these days, if you know what I mean."

"We know." Emma smiled, apologetically.

"Okay, well, there's no easy way to say this, so I'll just say it." I stopped. I didn't know how to choose the right words. I stared down at Brylee's UGGs, fixating on them. They were black and looked brand new, perhaps a Christmas present.

"V? What is it already? Out with it. I don't have time for your dramatics," Brylee said, putting her hands on her hips.

"Brylee, what can you tell us about Cory?"

"My brother? What does he have to do with this? What are you even talking about? The next words out of your mouth better make sens—"

"We saw Cory talking to Pedro today," Emma blurted.

"What? That's not possible." She crossed her arms.

"Yeah, I'm sorry, but it is," I said. "Actually, did you know he's in our Driver's Ed course? Mr. C said something about it being his last day, but he drove first. And I got the impression he knew who we were. He kept staring at me in the rearview mirror."

"What the hell?" Brylee's brows furrowed. "What's going on?"

"You didn't know?" I asked.

"No, I didn't know!" she spat. "Cory has been away at boarding school for the last five years. He only comes home for holidays, summers, and the occasional extended weekend. And most summers, we're usually all shipped off to my dad's ranch in Argentina. Cory doesn't talk to me much about anything. Mom told me he got caught cheating on a test last month and was expelled. My stepdad was able to get him into another private school locally. He's going to be living at home with us for the first time since he was ten years old. Let's just say, he hasn't made the best choices."

"Is that why you've never talked about him?" Emma asked.

"What is there to say? My brother is the black sheep of the family. Our father was hoping he'd take an interest in his cattle ranch someday and move back to Argentina to go into the family business. But we all know that's never going to happen. He makes C's and D's in school and barely gets by. His friends are losers—rich, prep school assholes who don't care about him. They just use him to do their dirty work for them, like stealing tests. I had no idea he was even driving, let alone in a Driver's Ed course. Good for him. If he passes, it'll be the first thing he ever finished without messing it up. But wait, Pedro? Why and how would he ever talk to Pedro?"

"We don't know," I admitted, "but I spotted them behind the dumpsters at Milo's. It looked like they knew each other to me. Pedro was talking to him, even laughing. But I couldn't hear what they said."

"Leave it to my brother to find the only trouble around here the second he gets back. He's been warned that if he messes up one more time, he'll be shipped off to military school. He's an idiot."

"Maybe he doesn't know who Pedro is?" Emma said.

"Yeah right. Save it," Brylee huffed. But I saw the concern etched in her eyes.

"Will you take the case again, V?" Emma asked. "Now that Cory's involved?"

"What? I ... uh ..."

OFFICE

29

PERSPECTIVE

It was now Wednesday, fourth period Honors Chemistry, and we were about to watch Mrs. Harrington blow something up. I tried not to think about Brylee's brother being mixed up with Pedro and his gang, tried not to think about Mr. C still transporting stolen stuff for them, and definitely tried not to think about Brylee's and Emma's pleas that I take the case again. I just wanted to live a normal, drama-free life. Was that too much to ask?

So I cleared my mind the best I could and watched with my classmates while Mrs. Harrington set up an assortment of colorful beakers of chemicals and liquids. Just as she was about to get to the good part, a student walked in and handed her a note. She thanked her, read the note, and said, "V, you're wanted in the office."

Great. Now what. I was going to miss the best part. Mrs. Harrington's mad chemist explosions were legendary. Reluctantly, I picked up my backpack and headed to the office, wondering what I did this time.

I walked in the office to be greeted by Suzie. She handed me a folder and told me to "hurry and shove this in your backpack. And you better memorize it or do whatever you have to with it during lunch and then give it back to me. If anyone looks for it and discovers it's missing, I'm throwing you under the bus."

I'd nearly forgotten I'd asked her to get me Crash's file. Now that I had it, did I really want to know what was in it? "Thanks," I muttered. "I owe you one. I'll meet you in the library at the end of lunch."

She nodded and told me Dr. Sykes was expecting me.

I TAPPED on her partially open door.

"Come in, V," Dr. Sykes said.

"What's up?" I slung my backpack over the back of the chair in front of her desk and dropped into it, leaning back.

She smiled at me and waved toward the chair. "Make yourself comfortable. You're in a good mood."

"Not really, but I'm learning to 'fake it till ya make it.' So, why am I here?"

"It's just a formality, a required follow-up to check in with you. It's been a while since your last appointment, and since you waived any off-campus counseling or therapy, it's my job to make sure you're okay."

"I'm good. Never better. In fact, I had a wonderful Christmas with my family, and we even got to see some snow."

"Really?"

"Yep, we went to Joshua Tree. It snowed about an inch and melted the same day, but it was magical."

"That sounds lovely," she said, smiling.

"Indeed. It was," I replied.

"So what's bothering you?"

"What makes you think something's bothering me?"

"Because you said, 'not really,' when I asked about your mood."

"Oh. Right."

"V, you can tell me. That's what I'm here for, remember?"

"Is Brylee's therapy going well?" I blurted it out before thinking about the consequences.

"You know I can't talk to you about another patient. Why do you ask?"

"I just want to make sure she's getting the help she needs. She . . . she's been through a lot, and I want to make sure she's okay."

"I'd have to talk to her therapist, and even then I'm not sure she'd tell me. What Brylee says in those sessions is confidential, between her and her therapist."

I nodded.

"The last report I got was that she was making good progress," she added, as if to reassure me. But then she said, "V, did something happen? Is Brylee engaging in self-harm?"

"What? No, nothing like that. She broke up with her boyfriend, that's all. Just normal, teenage stuff. Never mind, I'm sure she's fine. She'll be fine. Forget I said anything."

"You'll tell me if you notice signs of depression or suicidal tendencies, right?" She reached in a desk drawer and pulled out a pamphlet. "Here, take this. If she shows any of these signs, call me right away. Even if it's after hours. Here's my personal cell." She wrote her number on the pamphlet and handed it to me just as the bell rang, signaling lunchtime.

I took the pamphlet and stood up to leave. "I'm sorry, Dr. Sykes. I didn't mean to worry you. I overreacted, that's all. Like I said, she'll be fine. She has Emma and me." I grabbed my backpack and left before she had a chance to stop me. *What was that stuff about self-harm? I think Dr. Sykes told me more than she realized. And Brylee might be in more trouble than I thought. I have to tell Emma.*

I HAD twenty minutes to go through Crash's file before lunch ended, which meant I couldn't think about Brylee right now. I took a giant bite of my peanut butter and banana sandwich on my way to the restroom and then locked myself in a stall in the girls' bathroom and pulled the file out of my backpack. No one could see me with a student's file; it would be bad for me, but worse for Suzie. *Well, I might as well get this over with.*

The file was a mess, records from this school and his old schools all jumbled together, with handwritten notes from past teachers and school counselors. I snapped a couple shots of the background stuff and flipped through the rest of the file quickly, noting his practically perfect record: nearly straight A's, no detentions or disciplinary actions, nothing. I couldn't figure out why he'd transferred here last year. Or why I assumed he'd done something wrong at his other school. And then I saw it, the reason his family had moved here:

Zackery Albert Collins, birthdate February 20, 2001. Mother, Chloe, is a dental assistant and father, Al, is a general contractor. Written in pencil in the margins,

> *Zack is biracial: black mom, white dad, one sibling. Parents divorced last year.*

There was a note from a counselor at his old school:

> *Zack is a bright young man. He's kind and sweet and seems to be taking his parents' divorce well, under the circumstances. But since he skateboards to and from school, I worry about him falling into the wrong crowd, especially since his mother's late hours due to commuting from LA to Orange for her new job. I recommended this transfer to a high school near his mother's new job, along with a list of housing prospects for Zack and his mother. It will be a fresh start for the family.*

CRASH NEVER TOLD me his parents divorced. Or even that he had a sibling. But then again, I guess I never gave him the chance. Every time he tried to get to know me or make small talk, I shut him down. Why would he tell me something like this? According to the file, they lived in East LA before moving to Orange. Crash transferred here at the end of October last year . . . and the first thing he did was crash into my mom with his skateboard. And the first thing I did was try to beat up the new kid. I felt like a terrible person. Why would he be so nice to me? I definitely didn't deserve it.

I closed the file and found Suzie in the library, just like we'd agreed.

"Did you get the dirt on your bad boy?" she asked.

"Uh, yeah, I guess," I managed.

"What's the matter? Is Zack not such a bad boy after all?"

"You could say that."

"It's amazing what you might find out about a person if you just take the time to get to know them a little, don't you think?" Suzie grinned up at me.

"What's that supposed to mean? How do you know Zack?"

"I don't. But not everyone is out to get you, V. I think Zack just has a harmless crush, that's all. Let him down gently."

"Right. Thanks, Suzie."

"Sure." She stood up to leave. "But, V?"

"Yeah?"

"Remember, you owe me one."

30

I'M THE ONE NEXT TO THE PRETTY GIRL

Since I didn't have Driver's Ed after school, I decided to find out a little more about Cory. Emma had a soccer game, and Brylee had track practice, so I was on my own. But I was cool with it—that was how I worked best anyway. When Brylee told us about her brother, she and Emma pleaded with me to take the case again, the case I'd promised Santi I'd crack open that would put Pedro behind bars and free him. Now Cory was involved, too. This sucked. I was still afraid of Pedro and what he could do to me and my family, but if I did nothing, he was likely to hurt my friends and family eventually, anyway. He knew I knew too much, and I was a loose end, wasn't I?

I hadn't fully decided I wanted to do this, but if I was careful, at least I could check it out. I walked to the park near school and called an Uber. If Santi or anyone in the gang saw an Uber driving around, they wouldn't care. I didn't know where Pedro lived or where his gang's hideout was, or whatever they called it, but I remembered the strip mall Santi had taken me to a few months ago. I knew he made drops there of their stolen stash. I figured it was as good a place as any to start.

I looked up cigar shops in the area and found one nearby. Hopefully it was the right one. I plugged in my destination and saw there was an Uber two minutes away. A minute later, the Uber driver called me.

"Hello?"

"I just wanted to confirm I'm in the right pickup spot. You're standing next to the pretty girl with the Afro on your right; is that correct?"

I looked over to my right and saw the girl the driver was talking about. "Yeah, how did you know?"

"Because you're the only one in the area on the phone, and I can read your lips." She pulled up to the curb, and I got in. She already had the address I'd entered into the app and quickly pulled away without saying hello or acknowledging me. Since this was my first Uber ride, I wasn't really sure what to expect.

I wondered why she had described the person next to me and not me when confirming the ride. And she'd described the girl as "pretty." *Interesting. Clearly I'm not her type!* I laughed to myself.

When the driver pulled up to the strip mall, she said, "Where to?"

"What?"

"Where should I drop you?"

"Oh, um, can you just park up there for a couple minutes? Is that okay?" I pointed to an empty row of parking spaces near the cigar shop.

"Sure, but I can't turn off the meter until you get out of the car."

"No problem. I just want to have a look around, then I want you to take me—"

I stopped midsentence. I couldn't believe it. I saw Santi and Cory walking toward the parking lot, an empty duffel bag in Santi's hand. They got in a beat-up white Honda and drove away.

"Follow that car," I said, pointing.

"Look, kid, I don't really do that."

"I'll pay you double."

"Here we go."

She followed at a safe distance, staying back when Santi made a turn, and then turning a few car lengths later. *Hmm, I wonder if she's done this before.*

Santi turned right onto a long residential street. Instead of turning where he turned, the driver pulled over. We could still see his car from the street corner. About halfway down, he pulled into a driveway. He and Cory got out.

I waited until they went in the house and then asked the driver to go slowly past the house. I snapped a pic of the front of the house as we drove by. A few houses down, I asked the driver to pull over. The house was small, a dirty-white stucco in need of repairs. I wondered who lived there.

After a few minutes, the driver said, "How long do you want to wait here? You know this is gonna cost more, right?"

"Oh, right. Sorry. You can take me home now."

"Who are you spying on, anyway? Your boyfriend?"

"Something like that."

WHEN I GOT HOME, I did a Google search of the address to see if it would tell me who owned the house. No such luck. "Now what?" I said to my empty room.

I had a lot to think about. I decided to make a list. Let's call it a mind dump, of sorts. I got a pen off my desk, took my journal out of its secret hiding place from behind my bookcase, and plopped onto my bed. I opened the journal and began to write.

WHAT I KNOW/LEARNED:
Brylee might be harming herself
I have to tell Emma for Brylee's safety
Crash isn't a bad guy
Crash hasn't had it easy
Crash's parents are divorced
I've been too hard on Crash
Cory is definitely in Pedro's gang
I have to help Brylee!
I have to help Cory if I can
I have to solve this case

WHAT I WANT TO KNOW:
Who lives in the house Santi & Cory visited?
How did Cory get involved so quickly?
(He just got back from boarding school!)
Has Pedro ever killed anyone?
(Do I really want to know this??)
Where is Pedro's hideout?
Is that even what they call it?
Why has Crash been so nice to me?
(I've treated him terribly!)
Why can't I stop thinking about Crash?

DO I HAVE FEELINGS FOR CRASH?

I slammed the journal shut, exasperated. *This is getting me nowhere.*

31
MR. C

"How's school going, V?" Mom asked at dinner.

"Fine. Why?" I tried to sound casual.

"I heard that you saw Dr. Sykes today."

"Isn't that supposed to be privileged? You know, confidential between me and my counselor?"

"Yes, I know what privileged means. She didn't tell me what you talked about, and she only brought it up in conversation. Why are you so defensive? I'm just checking in with you. It's our first week back at school after Christmas break. I'm your mom. It's what I do. I care. Sue me."

"That's funny, Mommy!" Scotty chimed in, laughing. "Sue me! Hahaha!"

I glared at Scotty but couldn't help myself. I laughed, too. I needed to relax. Mom and Dad didn't know the weight-of-the-world thoughts that were swirling in my head. We finished dinner, and I pretended everything was great, smiling, joking, and laughing with my family.

After I cleared the table, rinsed the dishes, and put them in the dishwasher, I said I had to finish my homework. I excused myself and went upstairs to my room. As soon as I got there, I texted Emma.

> I need to talk to you!

Sry can't talk now… pizza party w/team. We won!!!!

> Congratulations! That's great! When can we talk?

I hav HW tonight. After school tomorrow? During Drivers Ed?

> OK. Bye.

Bye

I didn't want to wait to tell her about Brylee, but I guess I had to. I also wondered if I should tell her about my conflicting emotions over Crash. Emma had never had a boyfriend. Technically, I hadn't either. But we'd never talked about crushes or guys we thought were cute. As far as I knew, Emma didn't even notice guys *in that way*. She was so driven with soccer she didn't seem to care about much else.

I had trouble sleeping that night and was awake when my alarm went off at six o'clock the next morning. I'd had the strangest dream about Crash. *This is getting ridiculous!*

* * * *

I SMILED AND SAID, "HI," to Crash when I walked into Computer class.

He stared at me, mouth gaping open. "Is this the same V who told me to get lost yesterday?"

"Yeah, sorry about that. I've had a lot on my mind lately. It's not you; it's me, and all that."

"Ha ha."

"No, really. I'm sorry. Truce?"

"Uh, yeah, okay."

I went to my seat and glanced back over my shoulder as I sat down. He was still looking at me, a dopey grin on his face.

Wow. How did I not see this before?

When class ended, Crash waited for me by the door. "Want to eat lunch together today?"

"Whoa, hold on there, Romeo," I said, winking. "Sorry, but I have to finish an assignment for AP Euro. It's due after lunch today, fifth period. I fell asleep last night before I could finish it," I lied.

"Oh. Uh, what about after school then?"

"Driver's Ed, remember that?"

"Yeah, how is ol' Mr. C anyway? I'm so glad I don't have to do that anymore. Hey, my birthday's next month. I'll be sixteen and can get my driver's license."

"Good for you. I've got a ways to go. My sweet sixteen isn't until June 24th." *Ugh. Why did I just tell him my birthday?* I had to leave before I said something else stupid. "Well, I better get to English before Miss Torres has a fit."

"Yeah, me, too. I mean, I have to get to my AP Euro class. Later."

"Later."

✦ ✦ ✦ ✦ ✦

AT LAST, school was out. I was in Mr. C's ugly car with Emma. It was my turn behind the wheel. Unfortunately, I hadn't had a chance to talk to her about Brylee yet because I couldn't find her right after school, and then I had to go to the meeting spot for Driver's Ed. Mr. C was already there when I got there, and Emma showed up a few minutes late. I gave her a quizzical look, but she just shrugged. She climbed into the back seat, and I got in the driver's seat, adjusted the seat and mirrors, and put on my seat belt.

After Mr. C gave me a few more simple instructions, he wanted me to practice parallel parking a few times. Finally, he had me take the car out on the freeway. I merged without slowing down and easily changed lanes.

"Goodness gracious, V, you're a natural-born driver," Mr. C said, grinning. "Look at you, handling this car like a pro. Are you sure your parents didn't take you out a few times before you took this class? It's okay if they did. In fact, we encourage it."

"Nope," I said, not able to conceal my own grin, thinking of when I drove Brylee and Emma that night after the party. "Just a quick learner, I guess."

"Yes, indeedy."

I tried not to roll my eyes at how much of a dork he was. I continued following his instructions and driving around for about an hour when he said, you guessed it, "Okay, what do you two say we take a little break before letting Emma take a crack at it? How about we stop by Milo's and get some sodas?"

"Sure, Mr. C. Whatever you say," I said, hoping to see Cory at their usual 'stolen goods exchange' so I could confirm my suspicions about him. *Oh no, I haven't even told Emma about Cory and Santi yet.*

I drove to the Mini Mart and parked in front of the store.

Mr. C got out of the car and walked into the store with us. I stopped, confused. He'd never done that before. I turned around slowly and looked at him, still expecting him to realize his mistake and make up one of his usual excuses about getting gas, going to the bank, making a phone call, or whatever else he usually came up with.

Yet, true to his word, he went to the fountain drink self-serve station in the back and poured himself a coke. I got another candy bar. This time I got a Kit Kat and Emma got a bag of chips.

Just when I thought I was in some sort of altered reality, that maybe Mr. C had finally quit working with Pedro's gang after all, a big, loud car pulled up outside next to Mr. C's car. Three guys got out of the car. One of them opened the driver's door of Mr. C's car and took the keys out of the ignition. He opened the trunk and took something out of it. I looked at Mr. C, stunned. He looked surprised, too.

He ran outside, and Emma and I watched from inside the store. In his haste, Mr. C left the door open, so Emma and I could hear them.

"Hold on there, young man. Just what do you think you're doing with that car?" Mr. C said—quite bravely, I thought.

"Hey, it's me, Mr. C; it's Cory. I needed to make a pickup. I heard you had a little something for me. No worries. Here ya go." He took a step toward Mr. C and tossed the keys to him.

"Cory? I don't understand. I didn't know you were with Pedro. Where is he?"

"Nah, that's where you're wrong, old man," another guy said.

"I'm sorry, have we met?" Mr. C asked. "Who are you?"

"Yeah, old-timer, you're gonna be sorry," the guy said. He grabbed Mr. C and held him while the third guy hit Mr. C over the head with the butt of his gun. Together, both guys picked up Mr. C and put him in the back seat of their car.

"Diego, what did you do that for?" Cory asked. "I had it under control."

"He's a witness, you idiot. You said there wouldn't be any witnesses, and I don't need no loose ends. Now get in the car or do I have to knock you out, too?"

I gasped and jerked Emma down, behind a magazine rack.

"Hey!" She pulled her arm away.

"Shh! I don't think they saw us. We have to be quiet."

"What's going on?"

"Shhh! I can't tell you now," I whispered. I motioned for her to stay there and stood up to peer out the window again. I was shaking. I couldn't believe I was seeing Diego, gang leader of La Palma 91, and Pedro's rival. From the police file I read, Diego was even scarier than Pedro. *What is Cory doing with Diego?*

Diego slammed the back door shut. "Huey, you drive. Cory, get in the back and babysit your friend. Let's go!" He opened the front passenger door and got in. There was more shouting but I couldn't make out what they were saying. I watched helplessly as the car peeled out of the parking lot—with an unconscious Mr. C in the back seat.

"Was that a 1964 Chevy Impala? What a beaut. What the hell was that all about?" the Mini Mart store clerk said, staring out the door.

"I don't know, but they kidnapped our Driver's Ed teacher," I said. "You better call the police. Emma, hurry, we have to go!"

"Are you nuts? You want to chase after them? How? Was that Cory? V, what's going on?" Emma trembled.

"Mr. C dropped the keys when Diego knocked him out. Look!" I pointed to the keys on the asphalt while running toward them. I grabbed the keys, got in the car, and started it, yelling for Emma to get in or get left behind. She jumped in, and I pushed the gas pedal all the way down, causing the tires to spin. I silently prayed I wouldn't get us killed with my driving.

Amazingly, I caught up to them. For one, I could hear their muffler a mile away. Plus, they got stuck at the notoriously long red light a couple blocks down from the Mini Mart. The problem was, I knew they'd recognize Mr. C's car, so I couldn't follow too closely and risk them seeing me. There were three cars between us.

"Whirr," a siren sounded. I looked in the rearview mirror and saw the police car behind me. I'd been so focused on not losing Diego, I never looked behind me. I knew I'd been speeding. This was terrible.

I pulled over and rolled down my window. How I'd talk myself out of this one, I had no idea. I watched in the side mirror as the officer approached the Driver's Ed car.

"I realize you're just a student driver, but do you know what the legal speed limit is here?" the officer asked while walking up to the car. "Wait a minute. V Jiménez, is that you? Oh my, we've got to stop meeting like this," Officer Alan Lomeli said, chuckling.

"Alan, Diego kidnapped Mr. C! We have to save him!" I screamed at him. "They're getting away! Hurry, get in!"

To my surprise, the young police officer got in the back seat. I floored it again. I glanced in the rearview mirror and met his eyes. Oddly, I saw trust. I felt the urge to explain the obvious, to fill the silence and ease the tension. "You understand why we can't take your police car, right? We're going to drive right up to where they're hiding and take them by surprise. A cop car will tip them off, and they'll kill Mr. C."

"I think you watch too many movies . . . but you might be

right. Still, I'm not comfortable bringing two civilians to a notorious gang leader's secret lair. It's way too dangerous, and two teenage girls at that. You two need to stay in the car. When we get there, I'll scout it out, find out how many bad guys we're up against, and call for backup."

I pretended to agree, and we rode the rest of the way in silence. I had to keep an eye on Diego's car without him spotting mine. Emma looked like she was going to be sick. When they turned into a salvage yard, I thought, *Wow, this really is like a movie.*

I pulled over and parked a block away. Alan got out of the car and warned us to stay there.

"Sure thing, Alan." I saluted him.

"It's Officer Lomeli to you. And I mean it, V. I don't care what kind of great detective you think you are. Stay in this car and let the professionals handle this." He pushed down the button to lock all the doors before shutting the driver's door, as if to lock us in for our own safety.

I laughed to myself. *Like that's gonna stop me.* I watched him walk away, then quickly turned to Emma. "Come on. I have a plan."

"What? No way! He just told us to stay here." She folded her arms across her chest and glared at me. "I'm staying here."

"Fine. But I'm going in. I think Cory's in big trouble."

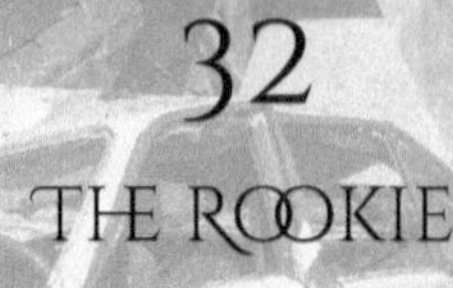

32

THE ROOKIE

I found a gap in the chain-link fence and slid into the salvage yard behind a tower of stacked cars. The place looked like a boneyard for cars with chunks of mangled metal and car 'skeletons' all around me. I tiptoed through metal scraps and scattered pieces of glass, careful not to make a sound, trying to get a good view.

I heard car doors slam and then scuffling sounds. I followed the sounds until I came across a clearing, of sorts. There was an open area among the piled-up cars, and in the middle was a big crane with a giant electromagnet. A car was stuck to it, suspended in the air. The crane operator stopped what he was doing in midmotion and sat there like a statue, with the car dangling. The guy's face was turned away, watching something. I looked toward what he was watching and saw them. The guy jumped out of the crane and ran away.

Diego half dragged Mr. C out of the car. He stumbled and looked dazed, his face ashen. Diego pulled him around to the back of the car and popped open the trunk. Huey grabbed Mr.

C while Diego pulled out guns and rifles from the trunk. He passed the guns out to two others, I assumed from his gang.

Cory was on the other side of the car with his back to me. I couldn't get a clear view to see what he was doing. I scanned the area for Officer Alan 'Rookie Cop' Lomeli, but he was nowhere in sight. *Hmm, interesting. I wonder if he chickened out after all.*

I stayed hidden, figuring I'd wait it out until they tied Mr. C up somewhere and left him alone. I'd swoop in, save him, and we'd run for our lives. Good plan, right? *But what about Cory? Think, V. Think.*

A hand grasped my shoulder. Instead of screaming, like every fiber of my being wanted to, I turned around and came face-to-face with Alan. He had one finger pressed to his lips.

"Duh," I mouthed. *Kudos to the rookie for sneaking up on me.*

He motioned for me to go back.

I shook my head.

He glared at me but seemed to accept that I wasn't going anywhere. He inched forward to get a better look as a big, loud lowrider car barreled through the salvage yard, stopping short of Diego's Chevy in the clearing. Pedro and his gang jumped out. I recognized Santi and Chewy, so the big guy had to be Javi. Using the car's open doors as shields, they started shooting before I even knew what was happening.

Mr. C, caught in the crossfire, and finding himself standing alone next to Diego's open trunk, flung himself into the trunk as a stray bullet careened past his ear. Another errant bullet tore through the trunk lid, the force of it causing the lid to close. Poor Mr. C was locked in the trunk in the middle of a gang war.

Alan whistled too loud. "That's a 1972 Plymouth Barracuda. Sweet."

"Shh! They'll hear you!" I whispered. Under my breath I added, "What is it with guys and big cars? My dream car is way cooler than that monstrosity."

He shot me a look and motioned for me to go down toward his right. Then he turned around and headed to the left, toward the battle and a melee of flying bullets.

I happily sprinted away from the shooting. I found a makeshift ladder and climbed up for a higher—and safer—view, atop some scaffolding. There, I found some hubcaps stacked in a neat pile on the scaffolding. I picked one up and felt the weight of it in my hands. I wondered if I could throw it like a Frisbee. I looked down at the scene before me, aimed, and flung the hubcap with force at one of Diego's guys, hitting him in the back of the head. He fell over, out cold. *Sweet.* I picked up another hubcap and lobbed it at Chewy, making sure not to hit Santi. Smack. He hit the dirt.

Pedro and Diego took turns hurtling insults and swearing at each other, shooting haphazardly. Bullets ricocheted off fenders and cars, but none came close to hitting their intended targets.

Alan saw what I'd just done, so he grabbed a hubcap and hurled it at a guy behind Diego's car. It bounced off the side of the car and into a pile of scrap metal. Diego whipped his head around, looking for the culprit. *Oh no, he's gonna see Alan!*

I picked up another hubcap and aimed it at Diego. He saw me out of the corner of his eye and turned, pointing his gun at me. Instead of throwing the hubcap, I dove off the scaffolding without thinking, to avoid being shot. I landed with a thud and twisted my ankle upon impact. I stifled a scream. *Ouch!*

At the same time, Alan grabbed another hubcap. This time, he threw it at Diego's hand, trying to knock the gun out of it. Instead, the hubcap veered past, hitting the crane and ricocheting between the crane and the lever. It hit the button on the lever, and a loud humming sound filled the area. Diego spun around and aimed his gun at Alan.

The crane came to life as the magnet released its hold on the cargo it possessed. Gravity took over, and the car dropped to the ground below.

Diego, still intent on killing Alan, suddenly looked up just in time to watch the magnet demagnetize above him, dropping a two-ton car on top of him. *Splat*. No more Diego.

The shooting stopped. Alan appeared at Pedro's side and whispered something in his ear. Pedro set his gun down and told Santi and Javi to do the same.

Diego's crew, realizing Pedro's gang was unarmed, turned and aimed their guns at Alan.

"Not so fast," Cory said, rifle pointed at Huey. "Put down your guns."

"Dude, what are you doing?" Huey spat. "You're with us!"

Just then, multiple police squad cars and a S.W.A.T. team pulled in and ascended on both gangs. A voice could be heard over a loudspeaker, "Freeze! You are surrounded. Drop your weapons and get down on the ground."

As the police began cuffing the criminals, reading them their rights, and loading them into the back of the squad cars, I searched for one of them: Santi. My eyes met his, and I watched silently as an officer led him to an awaiting police car. I wondered what would happen to him.

I then shifted my focus to Cory and noticed he was still uncuffed, walking around freely. I stayed trained on him as I sat still on the ground, holding my ankle.

Alan walked up to me and said, "You literally had to throw yourself into the fray? Didn't I tell you to stay put?"

"Sure, but I never listened to your uncle. What makes you think I'd listen to a rookie, Alan?"

"I told you, it's Officer Lomeli. And you should learn to respect the authorities."

"Okay, I will when I see someone with authority," I said, winking. "By the way, what did you say to Pedro to make him drop his gun like that?"

Alan smiled before he spoke, reflecting. "I took my sidearm out of the holster and put it in my jacket pocket during the gun battle. Just in case I got caught, I didn't want anyone grabbing for my gun. I also wasn't foolish enough to join in and just start shooting at them. So, I bided my time. When I threw that hubcap, I gave up my hiding spot. But as soon as Diego went down, I knew what I had to do. I circled around and snuck up behind Pedro. With one leader down, I knew all I had to do was subdue the other leader and the fight would be over.

"I placed my hands inside my jacket's pockets as I approached Pedro. I got real close, then leaned in close to his ear while placing the barrel of the gun in my pocket into his ribs. I cocked the gun. At the click, I whispered, 'Do you know what this is?' He nodded. Then, in a slightly unsteady voice, I said, 'As you can probably tell, I'm new to the force. And as you can probably tell, I'm scared about out of my mind, and this gun could go off by accident.' I didn't have to say another word. Pedro ordered his boys to put down their guns, and Cory took care of Diego's boys."

"What do you mean by, 'Cory took care of them'? Why weren't you afraid that Cory wouldn't shoot you himself?" I asked.

"Because Cory is a CI."

"A what?"

Alan laughed. "A confidential informant, a CI. He agreed to

infiltrate and inform on both gangs in exchange for immunity for his past crime."

"Immunity?"

"He won't be prosecuted for what got him expelled from boarding school."

"But how did he—"

"I'm afraid your questions will have to wait, V," Alan said. "You need to get that ankle looked at." He helped me get to my feet and half carried me to a waiting ambulance.

"I don't need an ambulance," I protested.

"Let them look you over and wrap the ankle," Alan said. "It probably just needs to be iced is all."

"Hello? Is somebody going to get me out of here? Please?" Mr. C's voice was faintly audible from the trunk of Diego's car.

"Mr. C!" I'd almost forgotten about him. "Someone has to help Mr. C!"

"It's all right, V. We got it." Alan asked Cory to jump in and escort me to the hospital, giving me a wink. He closed up the back of the ambulance and rapped twice. I was driven away before I had a chance to ask him anything else. But it was okay, because now I could pester Cory.

33
MISSING DIAMONDS

A few hours later, I sat on my bed with my ankle propped up under a couple pillows. It was just a minor sprain, and I'd be fine in a week or two. I'd have to be on crutches, but it was worth it. My parents were furious with me for playing teen detective again, naturally.

Emma and Brylee stopped by to see how I was. Emma was still a little shaken from being so close to a gang war. She said she had hidden on the floor of the back seat of Mr. C's Driver's Ed car, praying the whole time. She felt bad for freezing like that, but we all agreed she was definitely not cut out for detective work or law enforcement of any kind.

Brylee had a million questions about her brother, and I happily answered them all as I retold the story Cory had told me on the ride to the hospital. Even though we all knew my ankle wasn't broken, they'd had to take x-rays. Procedure, and all that.

"A few months ago, Cory got mixed up with a drug dealer at his fancy prep school. The guy had bullied him into selling drugs for him. Another student turned them in, and when Cory met with the prosecutor, he cut a deal and became an informant."

"What was the deal?" Brylee asked.

"I'm getting there," I said, losing patience. I wanted to relish this. "Our local police wanted Cory to befriend Diego's cousin, Huey, also a student at the prep school. He wanted Cory to keep an eye on Huey and report back anything he heard about Diego or any gang activity. The cousin was only there because his parents had sent him away when they found out he'd joined up with Diego's gang. Since Huey was the new kid at the school and didn't know anyone there, Cory said he'd been easy to make friends with.

"When Pedro took over here, the police wanted to close in, so they put pressure on Cory to get himself and Huey expelled and sent home. They wanted Huey to introduce Cory to his cousin Diego, gaining immediate trust into the gang. It worked. In fact, it worked so well that Diego asked Cory to pretend to join Pedro's gang to spy on him. Suddenly, he's under deep cover, in two gangs simultaneously, and informing on both.

"Today, Cory escalated things by bringing Diego to the Mini Mart. He didn't intend for Mr. C to get kidnapped. It was supposed to be him—meaning, he'd led Pedro to believe that Diego's gang was going to jump him. He was trying to start the gang war between Pedro and Diego, using himself as bait. It was risky, but if he did this, the police would clear his record and he'd be free to live a crime-free life. When Cory didn't show up at Pedro's, Pedro stormed Diego's turf with guns a-blazing. Expecting the ambush, with Detective Lomeli in his ear, Cory wore a wire and a bulletproof vest."

"Wait a sec," Emma said. "What do you mean Detective Lomeli was 'in his ear'? Wasn't he there, with you? I thought he didn't have an earpiece on him."

"No, Detective Lomeli is Andrew Lomeli, Officer Alan Lomeli's uncle. I can see how you'd be confused, but there's a pretty big difference between a police detective and a police officer, especially a rookie officer, so don't let them hear you say that."

Emma rolled her eyes. "It's more the two Lomelis that's confusing me."

"Then what happened?" Brylee asked, giving Emma a look.

"Sorry," Emma said. "Didn't mean to ruin the story."

"Then *Detective* Lomeli, the seasoned one, called in the troops at Cory's request for backup. And wouldn't you know it, they arrived in the nick of time."

"Where's Cory now?" Brylee asked.

"I don't know. He brought me here and then said he had to take care of something. He's probably reporting in at the station."

Brylee blinked at me, tears brimming. "So, my brother isn't a loser?"

"No, Brylee, he isn't," I said, smiling. "He saved Mr. C, the rookie cop, and me. Your brother is a hero."

THREE DAYS LATER, Detective Andrew Lomeli called me down to his office. "I hear you played cops and robbers with my nephew," he chided. "How many times do I have to tell you to leave the catching the bad guys to us?"

"I know you didn't call me in here just to scold me," I said. "What can I help you with, Detective Lomeli?"

"Don't get cute with me, young lady. You're lucky all you got was a twisted ankle. But from what Alan told me, you should enter a Frisbee throwing contest. Apparently, you can throw a mean hubcap with incredible accuracy."

I laughed. That was the closest thing to a thanks I'd ever get from Lomeli. I also smiled as I remembered the summer my dad taught me how to throw a Frisbee with a forceful spin . . . or "torque action," as he liked to call it. "It's all in the wrist," he'd say.

"So, I'll cut to it, then," Lomeli continued. "We found two loose diamonds tangled in the threading along the inside seams of a large duffel bag. After inspection by a jewel expert, the gems belong to a Simon G. 18K white gold diamond cluster necklace featuring 17.3 carats of princess-, pear-, and marquise-cut white diamonds. The necklace is one of a kind and worth $80,000. It is registered to Martina Thompson, Brylee Rossi's mother. You wouldn't happen to know anything about this, would you, V?"

I squirmed but didn't answer.

"You see, the necklace wasn't reported stolen, and it wasn't found with any of the stolen merchandise we recovered from both gangs and a cigar shop. But if someone were to, say, come forward as a witness and prove the necklace had been a part of this, we'd be able to tie the bag, with the gang's fingerprints all over it, to the burglaries as evidence. This connection would give us an airtight conviction to put these guys away for good."

"Yes, I can prove the necklace was stolen. I found it in Mr. C's trunk and gave it back to Brylee. She returned it to her mom's safe before her mom ever knew it was missing. I can get her to bring you the necklace and you will find there are two missing diamonds at the back of the necklace, near the clasp. They're the diamonds your people found. I'm 100 percent sure. But can we do this without alerting Martina Thompson? I don't want Brylee to get in trouble."

"She should have thought of that when she 'borrowed,' without asking, an 80,000-dollar necklace."

"Please. I can bring it to you myself. Don't you think Brylee's been through enough?"

"Oh, all right. Have it here first thing tomorrow."

34
LIFE GOES ON

Lomeli kept his word, and Mrs. Thompson's necklace was removed and returned to her safe, without her knowledge, with the loose gems securely back in their settings. Everything had been catalogued, photographed, checked for prints, and entered into evidence. They no longer needed the physical proof.

Mr. C and Santi both got reduced sentences for their full cooperation in telling the police everything they knew about Pedro's organization. Pedro, Javi, and Chewy went to prison for a long time. So did Diego's gang: Felipe, Arturo, and Huey. Cory was completely exonerated and returned to his fancy prep school. He decided to keep his nose clean and planned to graduate with honors in the hope of joining the CIA someday.

Me? Well, Emma and I completed our Driver's Ed course at another driving school, paid for by the Orange Police Department since they had to shut down Dan's Driving Instruction. We were his only two students anyway.

Brylee admitted she suffered from depression and said she'd cut herself on purpose a few times. Her parents sent her to a treatment facility where she was able to take online courses for the remainder of her senior year and, we were told, would still be able to graduate on time.

And my family? I'd love to tell you all is well there, too. But sadly, that is not the case.

LESS THAN TWO weeks after the gang war, January 17th, Mom and Dad went to a routine doctor appointment. Or, at least I thought it was routine. Mom called me into her bedroom to tell me the news.

"Sweetie, I have some rough news to tell you."

"What is it, Mom?" I asked.

"I had a bad scan, and it looks like the cancer is back. Dad and I will see a thoracic surgeon on Monday to schedule a biopsy and another surgery."

"No! It's not! I don't believe it! It's not ever supposed to come back. But even if it did, it's way too soon!"

"I'm so sorry, sweetheart. I'm still in shock, too. I truly thought I beat it. I thought I would at least get a few more years in before having to do this again."

"Mommy, nooooo. You can't be sick. This is terrible." I sobbed into my mom's shoulder as she held me.

"I'm so sad, too, honey. But you know me. I'm a fighter. I will get it together and fight this with everything I have!"

"I know you will, Mom," I said, sniffling. I pulled away from her embrace and gave her my bravest smile. "I know you will," I repeated. It was all I could say.

35
ZACK COLLINS

Crash finally convinced me to go on a date with him —well, a study date anyway. Mr. Feta announced a big test in AP Euro the day after I found out my mom's cancer was back. I got through my classes on autopilot, barely registering Crash in the hall after school.

"Hey, V," Crash said, walking up to my locker.

"Hey, Crash. What's up?" I asked, still thinking about my mom.

"Are you ready for the big AP Euro test this Friday?"

"Nope. Not even close."

"I could help you study."

"Okay."

"Really? I mean, cool. It's a date. I mean, not a date. It's a study date. So, anyway, want to meet at the library tomorrow after school?"

"Sure, okay."

"Awesome! See you tomorrow!" Crash waved, smiling broadly before turning around and walking away.

"Yeah, see you tomorrow," I said, waving back. *What did I just agree to?*

At the library the next day, Crash actually came up with a great system to help me remember dates in history. We finished filling out the study guide, quizzed each other a few times, and he even helped me with some math homework. After that, he offered to walk me home. I told him about my mom's cancer coming back, and he told me about his parents' divorce. Then he told a bunch of lame jokes and had me laughing all the way home.

On Friday, he took the test second period and told me it was easy, that I knew the material, and that I had nothing to worry about. I studied a little more at lunch to make sure I felt confident. When I took the test fifth period, I felt good about it. By the time I checked after school, Mr. Feta had already entered the test grades for all periods. Crash and I both aced it! I couldn't believe it.

Crash said we *had* to celebrate. He asked me out on a real date that night.

TWO WEEKS LATER, Crash and I had seen or at least talked to each other every day since our first study date. We'd been taking it slow. We hadn't even kissed yet. But tonight felt different. He'd been there for me when my mom's surgeon gave us more bad news after her biopsy. He helped me process my feelings. He was so easy to talk to. He held me when I cried.

And now, as he sat across the table from me at Cali Tacos, his beautiful, handsome face turned serious. His mouth formed a straight line, and his dimples nearly disappeared.

"I love you, V," Crash said softly, his blue-green eyes piercing my soul.

I stared at him, not sure what to say. Finally, I said, "You love *me*? Why? How? It's only been two weeks."

"You don't even know what you do to me, do you?"

"What are you talking about? You're crazy," I tried to joke, wanting to keep it light.

"Am I? Perhaps. But I know I'm crazy in love with you."

"I don't believe you." I squeezed my eyes shut, willing away the tears. *Stupid emotions.*

"Okay, let's see if I can sort out my feelings logically. . . . Hmm . . . how can I love you even though it's only been 'two weeks,' or so you say? Why do I love you? That's easy. I fell in love with you over a year ago, the day I ran into your mom with my skateboard and you were so protective of her that you wanted to punch my lights out. I love that you love your mom and want to ferociously protect her. I love that you stand up for your beliefs and you don't take crap from anyone. I love that you're so fearless you boldly rush into the face of danger without a thought for your own safety, flying through the air like Captain Marvel! Then you come out of it practically unscathed with only a minor ankle injury. I love how beautiful you are—the natural beauty that shines through you, even when you try so hard to shut everyone out. You have a beautiful heart, V. You are a beautiful person. And it's time you knew that. I loved you when you knocked me over when my drone crashed on the first day of school. And I love that you stubbornly refuse to call me by my real name, clinging to a silly nickname to avoid getting too close." He stopped talking.

He reached across the table and took my hands in his, gazing into my eyes before speaking again. "I love everything about you, V. I just love *you*."

I swallowed hard, feeling my heart thud against my chest. I locked eyes with him, trying to sort out what I should say. No, not what I *should* say, but what I really wanted to say, what I felt and had denied for so long. I took a deep breath and removed my hands from his.

He frowned.

"It's okay," I said. "My hands are sweaty, that's all."

"Don't keep me in suspense! V, you're killing me here."

"Sorry. Um, it's just that, I don't know what to say. This is so unexpected. I need time to—no, scratch that. I have feelings for you, too. I do. I mean, I think I might love you too . . . Zack." I let the tears cascade freely down my face. And I couldn't stop smiling.

"You *might* love me?" he teased. "Well, that's a good start."

THANK YOU

As a thank you for reading *Bright Stars* I'm gifting you Brylee's short story, "Running in the Rain" as a free download on my website. You'll also receive the original short story, "The Legend of the Glass Stars," as well as updates on new releases. Just go to my website at taschelaine.com to signup.

If you enjoyed this book, will you please do me a favor and post a review for *Bright Stars* on Goodreads, Amazon, or your favorite bookseller or review site? A review is the best gift you can give an author.

V, her friends and I thank you!

Acknowledgments

I would like to express my deepest appreciation to my editor, Allison Rose, of Purple Rose Editing. I am grateful for her amazing ability to spot the tiniest error! I would also like to extend my deepest gratitude to my talented cover designer at 100 Covers (100covers.com).

I'm immensely grateful to Tiana for her sage advice and invaluable insight into "teen-speak," keeping my clichés to a minimum and my references current.

I would also like to extend my sincere thanks to my ARC team for their early reviews and help with getting this book out there! I'd be lost without them!

A big thank you to Jas List for her expertise on the inner workings of dog rescues and explaining the process to me. Also, thanks to everyone at OC POM Rescue (ocpomrescue.com) for the amazing work you do with rescue dogs, saving lives daily!

This book would not have been possible without the unwavering support and nurturing of my husband, Peter Valdez (even though he'll probably never read this!). Thank you for feeding me and making sure I took adequate rest breaks now and then, prying my fingers off the keyboard when warranted. Love you, honey!

Thanks also to Peter for his extensive knowledge of latino gangs in LA and for helping me with my research. Hopefully I added some realism to a fantastical story.

Finally, a special thanks to you, the reader. I hope you have enjoyed V's story so far, and that you continue her journey with me as we finish the series.

About the Author

 Tasche Laine has worked as a journalist, teacher, and book editor. Her published works include book award winners *CLOSURE* and *CHAMELEON*, two short story anthologies: *Winds of Winter* and *Wings of Prophecy,* and the young adult mystery series, *CHRONICLES OF V*. She also co-writes a children's book series, *Lil Peter,* with her husband, Peter Valdez.

Tasche grew up in a small town in Oregon, has lived all over the U.S., and currently lives in the Pacific Northwest with her husband and their puppy, Story. She visits family in southern California often—whenever she needs a sunshine boost. For more information, please visit her website at taschelaine.com.

facebook.com/TascheLaine

instagram.com/tasches

amazon.com/author/taschelaine

goodreads.com/tasche_laine

bookbub.com/authors/tasche-laine

ALSO BY TASCHE LAINE

CLOSURE: Based On A True Story

CHAMELEON: A Domestic Thriller

SHORT STORY COLLECTIONS

WINDS of WINTER

WINGS of PROPHECY

CHRONICLES OF V

GLASS STARS

BRIGHT STARS

BROKEN STARS (coming soon!)

FOREVER STARS (coming soon!)

CHILDREN'S SERIES

Get Up, Lil Peter. Get Up!

You Can't Quit, Lil Peter, You Just Can't

Teamwork, Lil Peter, It Works

Pick Me, Lil Peter, Pick Me

Small Things, Lil Peter, Make A Big Difference

Smile Lil Peter, It's A Gift